Undeveloped Memories

by

Karina Bartow

Cover Art by *Lisa Dawn MacDonald*

The Wild Rose Press, Inc.
PO Box 708
Adams Basin, NY 14410-0708
Visit us at www.thewildrosepress.com

Publishing History
First Edition, 2025
Trade Paperback ISBN 978-1-5092-6290-8
Digital ISBN 978-1-5092-6291-5

Published in the United States of America

Dedication

To Mari & all survivors of the 1964 earthquake

Prologue

1964

Reed Carmichael hoisted his blue tweed suitcase onto his bed and unfastened the zipper. He hadn't drunk a sip of alcohol, but the faint whiz of the metal teeth crashed in his mind as if he were hungover. The tiny, insignificant pulley slid across its track without any effort, oblivious of what its three-second journey meant to his life's trajectory. As it unlocked each clasp, his memories of the past two months—along with the dreams born during that time—ripped apart in similar succession. Like the inanimate object's one-way course, his future stood in front of him with a single path, and he couldn't turn back by his own accord.

Numb, he sorted through his clothes inside. He washed a load of laundry the day before, so most everything could go right into his closet. He emptied his thoughts while he performed the mundane task, blocking out the stories each garment could tell. He even sucked in his breath, not wanting to catch a whiff of the familiar scents remaining that would surely pierce his heart.

Being August in Sedona, Arizona, he wouldn't need any of the cold weather gear he packed for a while, so he stashed all the flannel and sweaters into a trunk. He questioned why he bothered to cart home the heavy insulated boots he purchased, given he never headed farther north than Flagstaff in the wintertime. Truth be told, snow grew on him along his travels, and under different circumstances, he'd seek it out more often from now on. Considering the emotions that the ice crystals would evoke, though, he planned to avoid cold climates with more fervor than ever.

His hazed state made the chore pass quickly, and he winced when he noted the stack of clothes had dwindled away. At the bottom of the case lay an envelope of photographs, alongside a canister of film. The roll it contained dwarfed all of his previous work, even if the shots on it wouldn't net him the accolades he used to prize. He didn't imagine they would meet the typical standards he set for his art, but he could only fathom the depths of his reverence for them. He once believed he loved photography that captured the unspoken messages of life and required contemplation to untangle them. In this instance, the prints would declare a message with sharp clarity. He just couldn't decide if he'd be able to bear having that message stare back at him.

He didn't touch the envelope or container but flipped the lid of the case closed and lay down beside it. He covered his eyes with his hands, shielding his view of his new reality. At this time yesterday, he was boarding the plane in Anchorage, Alaska, but that seemed like a lifetime ago now. He figured this unexpected homecoming would be tough, but the enormity of it didn't sink in until he faced the children. Within the course of forty-eight hours, he navigated two life-altering conversations, and he deemed himself ill-equipped for both of them.

The phone rang from the living room, jolting him out of his nostalgia and into protect mode. As he raced out to answer it, all he cared about was keeping his seven-year-old nephew and four-year-old niece asleep after the hard-won battle with the sandman. On just his first night with kids in the house, he already understood the reason for his brother's agitation when he called after eight.

He picked up the receiver on the second ring. "Hello?"

"How's everybody doing?" The kindness in Gabe Douglas' intonation made it difficult to be angry over his bad timing.

Even so, Reed stretched out the telephone cord into the hallway so he could peer inside the rooms to discern if the kids remained asleep. After he found them both still under the covers, eyes closed, he replied to his boss, "We're holding up. Harley's trying to convince me he's seventy instead of seven, acting like he's gone through this dozens of times. I expect he'll give me a run for my money, but I think he's putting it on for his sister. She's not handling it very well, but how could she? She's so much smaller than she looks in the pictures Jack and Audrey used to send."

Gabe stayed quiet, seeming to sense his vulnerability. During the silence, Reed glanced back in at Lorelei's small body, curled up beside her teddy bear. The nightlight next to her bed illuminated her face just enough to make out that the streaks on her cheeks left by her tears hadn't yet faded altogether.

"What about you?" Gabe finally asked.

Reed's mouth opened to speak, then closed, before he muttered, "I checked my emotional baggage along with my physical baggage at the airport yesterday, and I resolved not to collect it upon my return."

Gabe released a disbelieving chuckle. "Oh, did you

now?"

The comeback coaxed a grin to peek out of Reed's lips. "I appreciate that you gave me my job back."

"Well, I'm grateful you didn't decide to go to another journal. You still could've pursued deeper waters, although they might not be the ones you planned. I read your latest draft, and I know editors will be clamoring once you submit this and rack up the awards."

Reed shook his head. "That's not my aim anymore. Even before this happened, I decided not to go for it. I realize that was my original purpose, but it took on such greater meaning."

"I'll let you choose what's best, but don't be hasty about giving up on your dreams. I admire what you're doing here, but you deserve your own piece of happiness, too."

Reed thanked him for his supportive sentiments and told Gabe he'd be back to work the upcoming week. The conversation concluded, and he trotted to his room, taking one last gander into the kids' adjoining rooms. He contemplated what he'd lost in the previous five days— a dream, a brother and sister-in-law, and of course, the love of his life. While they all added up to a heavy toll, he considered these children's losses weightier. He couldn't fathom having his parents go to work and never make it home, not at the age of thirty-four, let alone during childhood. They missed out on years of their mom and dad's loving guidance and entered a strange home with the uncle they'd met on just a handful of occasions.

With those despondent thoughts swirling around in his head, he gazed once more at the suitcase holding the photos and film roll. Determined not to let anything prevent him from being who Harley and Lorelei needed, he zipped the suitcase shut again and carried it up to the attic. He set it down and descended the steps, refusing to dwell on the unattainable past and future it contained.

Chapter One

2014

Lorelei Carmichael gazed out of the plane and marveled at the red rock mountains of her hometown. Despite having viewed the landscape numerous times before, she still clutched her camera and snapped a few shots. All around her, her fellow passengers scrambled for their phones for the same reason, though the pilot hadn't yet given the go-ahead to use them. Like always, cries of fascination echoed through the cabin. She never tired of the collective wonder the Arizona mountains induced, especially among first-time visitors.

Once they landed, she retrieved her phone to learn what she missed during her five hours in the air. She wished she could delay the task for at least another few hours, as she considered it the worst part of the flight, but she needed to make sure her brother would be there to pick her up. Within moments, a message from Harley appeared, telling her he headed out from his ranch minutes ago. She estimated he'd arrive a tad late, but she didn't care. She didn't have a tight schedule for a change, and she could use some extra time to muster an ample amount of fortitude to face her brother.

Weaving her way through the busy Friday crowd, Lorelei decided to send a text to Uncle Reed, which would almost surely go unanswered. Her older uncle developed enough skills in technology to get by during his last couple of years of work, but he didn't make a habit of using modern-day communication. Still, she appreciated that he kept his phone nearby, given his poor health and recent history of falls. Now that Harley stuck him in a nursing home, he should be able to have assistance readily at hand, but Lorelei's experience of visiting other patients made her cynical of how speedy a response might be.

Uncle Reed proved her expectation wrong, replying that he couldn't wait to see her and even managed to add a smiley face. The gesture spritzed her with encouragement that Harley's grim reports about him may be exaggerated. Throughout the past three months, her brother continued to feed her stories about their uncle's worsening dementia and mobility issues. She agreed his diminishing physical stability called into question his safety in living alone, but she didn't put very much stock in Harley's assessment of his mental state. For years, Harley made knocks on Uncle Reed's sharpness, but when she was around, she didn't detect many of the signs her brother pointed out. Harley blamed her lack of observation on her absence, so she opted to take his trump card away by clearing her calendar and staying put for a while.

As she entered the baggage claim corridor, her phone rang, and she read Calvin Thompson's name on the screen. Her finger hovered over the decline button, not wanting a job offer from him that could test her resolution, but her passion for her work coerced her to answer. She just wished whatever opportunity the editor of Global Expeditions Magazine proposed would be nearby.

"Hi, Cal. What's up?"

"Good afternoon, Lorelei. I'm sorry for intruding on your trip. I realize your email last week said you wouldn't be available for several months, but I'm in a pinch. I assigned one of my guys to a major piece next month, but he's received a troubling diagnosis and can't make the journey. I could send another journalist, but we need this to be a visual masterpiece and would like it to have the mark of a renowned photographer. You're my top pick," Calvin told her.

Lorelei couldn't claim to be immune to the appeal of such pitches, as they stroked her ego and vindicated all the sacrifices she'd made for her career. In this instance, however, she couldn't allow flattery to crowd out her responsibility. "I appreciate that, but I can only help you out if it's close and quick. I have an obligation to my family."

"Well, I'm sure you could get what you need over a long weekend. The subject won't take you out of the country."

She sensed he was stalling. "It's a big country, Cal."

He snickered. "How foolish of me to try to outwit you. We're commemorating the fiftieth anniversary of the 1964 Alaska earthquake. We'd like to feature interviews with survivors, accented by some before and after visuals. In my biased opinion, your writing style and artistic eye would match this assignment perfectly. I'm ready to give you the compensation to prove that, too."

"If I wrote editorials, I'd whip up one right now about desperate men in positions of power. You'd make an ideal case study," she teased him.

"I couldn't pay you for that one," he replied, his manner playful.

Watching the first few suitcases finally appear on the baggage carousel, Lorelei considered the offer. She hated to renege on her word to Harley and Uncle Reed, but a payday like this would extend her sojourn in the long run. Plus, it'd help fund any needed renovations if she could check her uncle out of the care facility like she planned.

In the end, she took the open-ended route. "I need to evaluate how things are going around here before I can commit. Would you mind giving me a couple of days to mull it over?"

He agreed without hesitation and wished her a good homecoming. Moments after she hung up, she caught sight of her maroon hard-shelled luggage and strode over to grab it. She wheeled it up to the outside waiting area and sat on one of the benches so she could spot her brother. She didn't have to wait long for Harley, with his pickup truck soon crawling up the lane.

She stood and headed for the back of the bed, accustomed to the routine of hurried treks to and from the airport. Harley raised a fuss about a lot of topics, but to her gratitude, he never complained about giving her a lift home. They didn't share an emotional reunion, but deep down, she drew a sense of comfort from seeing his face before anybody else's, aside from Uncle Reed.

Harley performed his usual bit, stowing her luggage under the covered bed while she climbed into the cab. Once he secured everything, he joined her and drove off. Tension hung in the vehicle, as both of them were acquainted with the fact that this visit carried a greater purpose than her ordinary stays. Lorelei didn't keep her opinions about Uncle Reed's care a secret, and during their last serious conversation, she accused him of being selfish. He reciprocated by calling her a narcissistic gypsy, which stung. They exchanged apologies before the discussion wrapped up, but she fostered some hard feelings and reckoned he did, too.

She put forth an effort to overcome the strain. "Thanks for making yourself available. I'm sorry it had to be in the middle of the day. This was the only flight from Charleston, unless I landed in Phoenix."

"I don't mind. I'd rather be closer to home," he reminded her, as he had countless times. "I would've been more punctual if not for this."

She took the paper he plucked out of his shirt pocket, and the colors alone revealed what it was. In the past seven years, she held three other sonograms of his wife's. "Wow, big brother! You sure have made up for your late start into family life. Congratulations."

"Thank you. This one surprised us, but deep down, Viv always wanted four. They're monitoring her very close, but sixteen weeks in, everything's on the up and up. Of course, it's considered a geriatric pregnancy, but all of ours have been."

Lorelei giggled, given Genevieve was twelve years her junior. "If they term her geriatric, they would probably call me mummified."

Harley snickered, but his sister perceived anxiety in him. She wondered if he expected her to regret not having a family of her own, but she never indicated that. She didn't even want to analyze her true view on the matter. Rather, she just accepted that the route didn't open up to her as naturally as her career pursuits did.

Pondering his demeanor further, another explanation for it occurred to her. With Genevieve four months along, they would've learned of their new arrival around the same time Harley decided to admit Uncle Reed into the nursing home. All the dots lined up, providing a clear picture of his logic. Another baby meant more responsibilities, and something had to go. The elderly uncle who often taxed his nerves was an easy choice.

She drew in her indignation and refrained from charging him with the accusation. Nonetheless, he gave her added reason to be suspicious when he broached the subject of their uncle.

"Do you plan to head over to visit Uncle Reed this evening?"

"Yeah, I think I should have time after I drop everything off at home. When do they serve dinner?"

"Four-thirty."

Lorelei giggled, given they never ate before seven when they lived together. "I'll bet he loves that."

"I keep him stocked with snack cakes to have later so he doesn't go to bed hungry."

She thanked him, but the awkward mood between them set in again. Lorelei wondered if her knock on the facility's early suppertime activated his defense system, and she formulated the apology she'd mulled over during the flight. Before she could utter a word of the messy draft her brain had yet to complete, Harley cleared his throat and spoke.

"I didn't want to relay this over the phone, even though it probably would've explained some of my decisions. Uncle Reed's doctors have done a few tests because of his falls and other signs we've noticed, and they determined he's suffered several mini-strokes, which have affected his balance as well as some of his mental faculties. He changes day-to-day, with him seeming normal one day and very bad the next, so I want you to be prepared. When I dropped by last weekend, he wasn't able to speak at all, and the nurse told me that's happening more often lately."

Her protective guard assembled inside her all too quickly, provoking her to make a reply in her uncle's defense. Before she gave in to the instinct, she paused to gather her composure and endeavored not to elevate the temperature of the mood. "He always sounds like himself when I call. Even today, he responded to my text after I landed."

Harley's jaw squared with tension, but like her, he waited a beat to counter. "As I said, it's sporadic at this point. His main nurse and I are encouraging him to text more so he can communicate easier on those rough days. From what I've observed, he can form what he wants to say, but he struggles with how to get it out."

Lorelei had witnessed similar conditions in people throughout her travels, the most notable one being after a woman lost everything in a hurricane. Lorelei approached her and her family while they milled around the remnants of her house, but the poor lady remained mute through the interview. Her daughter admonished Lorelei not to take it as a personal affront, given she didn't utter a word in the wake of the disaster.

She didn't suspect tragedy lay behind Uncle Reed's regression, but Harley's report made her heart sink. She remembered meeting other stroke victims, including an uncle on her mom's side, and their frustration over their newfound limitations. Some cried when they tried and failed to perform a simple act. Her uncle always did everything on his own, and she couldn't fathom how he must feel about his diminished skills.

She kept quiet for the remainder of the journey to her childhood home, with a few tears springing from her eyes. Harley peered over when he parked in the driveway. "I didn't mean to hurt you in any of this. I realize, in your mind, he's still that strong man who gave us whatever we needed as kids. That's who I see when I look at him, too. But for his sake, we have to drop that filter and make realistic decisions. He did the same for us all our lives."

She nodded and mumbled that she understood, before she ducked out of the truck and collected her bag. With her shoulders drooped, she ambled across the rock garden that made up the front yard, noting the pesky weeds that sprouted up between the stones. Though Uncle Reed never excelled in landscaping, he hated weeds and ripped them out the instant a blade popped up. The tan stucco on the house was cracking in various spots on the façade, another indication of her astute uncle's—and negligent brother's—inability to keep up with the chores.

Lorelei fumbled around her purse for her keys, and once she located them, she selected the same one she'd used since her uncle gave it to her when she was eight. Upon opening the door, she basked in the familiarity, with the sights and aromas embracing her soul even though nobody occupied the space. A layer of dust blanketed the surfaces, but the warmness inside made her ignore it. The aggravation over the current circumstances abated for the moment, crowded out by the sentimentality that bubbled within her.

She rolled her suitcase over the threshold and sat down on the antique bench beside her, which belonged to her grandparents. She kicked off the boots she traveled in from Charleston, all the while remembering when Uncle Reed used to perform the act for her. The first time he did, her little legs barely extended past the pine seat, but they flailed with vigor. Meanwhile, he remained calm through her grief-induced tantrum and kept apologizing in response to her many complaints over his failure to do things like Mom and Dad. She'd never forget the gentleness in his green eyes when he made her the oath he held to ever since.

"Sweetie, I can't promise to do things the way your mommy and daddy did. They took care of you and Harley with the type of love only they can give you, and you showed love to them that you'll never give to anyone else, including me. But I can promise you that I will love you with a different kind that's still just for you, and I'll do whatever I can to show it to you every day. I hope you'll be able to do that for me, too."

The memory conjured up a few stray tears, as her gaze drifted to the photo on the wall of her with him and her brother at Harley's wedding. He stayed true to his words during every hardship they encountered as a family. He provided them with the utmost stability after their parents died in the fire at the restaurant they ran. Now, he struggled with challenges that transformed his life, reversing their roles. How could she not likewise measure out the special love she indeed developed for him?

****

After her initial nostalgia wore off, Lorelei couldn't afford to reminisce for very long, having to get the whole house into a livable state. Given she'd slept in an array of accommodations along her travels, she didn't mind the dust or clutter, but the lack of anyone's presence took its toll on the place. Harley switched off the power and water until that week, so she started her stay by checking on the appliances and utilities to make sure everything worked.

Once she confirmed there were no significant issues, she gave attention to the kitchen. Thankfully, her brother had enough sense to leave the refrigerator unplugged with the doors open, and not to her surprise, he emptied it along with every other cupboard, except the dishes and silverware. She understood the logic in not wanting the perishables to go to waste or invite vermin, but her survey uncovered other amenities that were missing. The air-fryer she bought Uncle Reed a few years ago no longer sat by the stove, and the single-cup coffee maker she gave him for his retirement had disappeared, as well. Considering how her brother and sister-in-law gawked when she presented them to him, she could deduce where she might find the cookware.

Lorelei shook away her ire and set off to secure what she needed for the first few days. She discovered Uncle Reed's car keys in their usual box atop the fireplace mantel, and she released a sigh of relief when the thirty-year-old SUV had both an operating battery and a full tank of gas. At least Harley drew the line of ethics short of grand theft auto.

She headed to Craig's Market for groceries and fought the temptation to dash across the street to the Thursday Morning store to shop for some home décor. She figured she'd better wait until she assessed how much Harley and Genevieve swiped before she replaced anything. She dropped her purchases off at the house before driving to Blissful Days Home. More than once, her brother used the nursing facility's name to persuade her of the facility's warm atmosphere, so she planned to test out his claims.

When she approached the building, she noted its similarity to the photo on the company's website. Black awnings accented the white exterior, but like everything in Sedona, the mountains behind it served as its best complement. Since she'd forgotten to ask if Uncle Reed's room faced the nearest formations, she made a mental note to pay attention. The facility appeared to be well maintained inside and out, featuring homey accents that helped the place seem less institutional. She didn't need to ask for Uncle Reed's room number, having sent several postcards to him since he was admitted.

As she observed the numbers getting close to his, Lorelei's ears picked up his voice, along with another familiar tone. She entered his doorway and spotted Gabe Douglas proving her suspicions correct. "Both my uncles in the same place. That's what I call convenient," she greeted them.

The men replied with happy welcomes. Lorelei strolled over to Uncle Reed first, with him in the bed. Even so, his skin radiated its usual tone, though the texture seemed coarser than she recalled. After offering him a hug and kiss on the cheek, she padded over to Gabe. Her uncle's longtime boss and friend was older than him by a few years, but Gabe remained independent and in good health.

He stood up with the aid of his cane and embraced his honorary niece. "What kind of groundbreaking story could this award-winning photojournalist do about two old farts like us?"

Uncle Reed laughed. "One about us falling on our faces and breaking ground."

"And breaking wind, while we're at it," Gabe added.

Lorelei chuckled along with them, shaking her head at how little the two had changed. From the time she and Harley moved to Sedona, just about every conversation Gabe and Uncle Reed had around her somehow led to flatulence…whether the circumstances merited it or not.

Once the boyish rowdiness retreated, Uncle Reed shifted toward her. "Gabe asked me what you covered in New York, but I couldn't remember."

"I was there for inauguration season. Between the mayor's and city council members', I attended fifteen in twelve days. Thank goodness I'm the one behind the camera so that nobody can snap a shot and shame me for wearing the same gown."

"Politicians won't pay any mind to what you have on as long as you capture what they have on from the right angle," Uncle Reed told her.

"Yeah, if they're two-hundred pounds overweight, it's only because you used the wrong lens and has nothing to do with all those fattening desserts they eat," Gabe said.

Uncle Reed motioned to his friend's portly belly. "And you don't know anything about those fattening desserts, do you?"

More razzing ensued between the guys, and Lorelei played observer, refreshed by it. She relished watching them act the way they always had, especially after the bleak picture Harley painted of their uncle. She failed to detect any of the signs he mentioned, as Uncle Reed made his typical counterblows to Gabe with ease. He never stammered in his speech or faltered over the memories they bandied about from decades ago. Still, her conscience reminded her that Harley acknowledged

Uncle Reed had his good days and bad, so she mustn't make a hasty conclusion based on today.

After a brief lull in conversation, Uncle Reed gave her a funny look but continued directing his words at Gabe. "Did I ever tell you about the first time I took the kids to the ocean?"

"Probably, but I'm not one to refuse a good story, and from the glint in your eye, I can tell it is," Gabe replied.

Lorelei agreed with the remark and debated which tale he would recite.

"After we all settled in together, I decided to take them to see the Pacific, beings they grew up on the Atlantic in Boston. We spent a week in Long Beach, and they had a blast. Harley really became fascinated with sand dollars and filled my camera case with them for the ride home."

Lorelei rolled her eyes, certain of the antidote now. "Even back then, he couldn't resist a dollar of any kind."

Uncle Reed chucked. "The boy realized how fragile the shells were, but his sister did not. To ensure their safety, he fed her this wild story that the little protrusion in the middle of them held a live dove. If you broke it open, of course, the bird would fly out and attack you."

Gabe cackled, before Lorelei chimed in. "Mind you, this wasn't long after Uncle Reed unwisely let us watch that horror movie about killer crows."

Uncle Reed wagged his finger at her. "His tactic worked. She wouldn't touch them, but you should've seen how she'd stare at his collection on the bookcase. You could almost hear the crazy scenarios reeling around in her brain. In fact, it's the same expression she's been leveling at me this whole visit."

Lorelei winced when he eyed her so squarely, and it took her a second to process his underhanded accusation. She didn't want to detail the claims Harley made about Uncle Reed's condition, even to indulge her childish urge to get him into trouble, so she kept her response simple. "What can I say? My big brother still likes to scare me."

"I don't think we ever outgrow sibling hijinks. To this day, my kids bicker like toddlers. Just wait till they read the will." Gabe winked, then changed the subject. "Your uncle tells me you're taking a hiatus from freelancing."

She nodded. "I built up a nest-egg to tide me over for a few months. I'm looking forward to a break."

Uncle Reed waved off the comment. "She says that now, but she'll be clamoring to go in a week. She shares the nomadic blood of her father, who never would've settled down if not for meeting Audrey. Plus, those editors won't quit calling her, given her talent. She probably already has her next offer waiting."

In truth, she feared Uncle Reed would feel guilty for detaining her if she revealed the Alaska proposition, but she also reckoned it would intrigue the men. "Global Expeditions Magazine wants to run a reflective article on the big Alaska earthquake since the fiftieth anniversary is coming up. They'd like me to consider going for them, but I'm inclined to pass."

"Well, if you opt to take it, you have a good resource right here." Gabe pointed to Uncle Reed.

"Really? Why's that?" she asked her uncle.

A foggy cast descended on Uncle Reed's face. Lorelei contemplated whether this was the start of an episode like Harley warned, but she sensed it stemmed from something even deeper than a physical defect. His voice sounded feebler when he spoke, "I'm too tired to explain it tonight."

She accepted his statement and interpreted it as a signal to let him rest. Gabe stood up to leave, too, and he offered his friend a contrite frown. After she hugged Uncle Reed goodbye, Gabe shook his hand and mumbled something. She couldn't be sure, but she thought he apologized and remarked that he wasn't thinking. She supposed he might be sorry for setting Uncle Reed up to show his worsening state, but how could he have predicted the random occurrence, if that's what it was?

Over the course of their enduring friendship, they must have secrets between them. Judging by the way Gabe roamed out to the parking lot beside her in uncharacteristic silence, Lorelei determined he just leaked one.

Chapter Two

Lorelei mulled over the puzzling end to her chat with Uncle Reed and Gabe during her journey home, but once she arrived, exhaustion drowned out her curiosity. While she unwound from her long day, she spotted an array of concerns she'd have to address around the place, but they could wait. Despite her uncle's adequate handyman skills, he often let projects go for a spell, so the incomplete odd jobs made his presence palpable.

She'd grown used to sleeping in unfamiliar territory because of the traveling her career entailed, but she always rested the best at Uncle Reed's. Since he kept the same mattress on her bed from her high school days, the foam didn't offer optimal comfort, but she could tolerate the aches it inflicted...at least when her stays were short. He preserved the décor, too, and although the peach walls with flower-power decals and teen idol posters didn't match her style anymore, they reminded her of the life he gave them.

As she lay underneath her polka-dot comforter, Lorelei reflected on Harley's comment about the image she had of her uncle. Did her reverence and gratitude for how he took them on blind her to his vulnerability? Did she elevate him above human status? She had trouble believing so, considering their share of arguments through the years. She and Uncle Reed remained closer than him and Harley, but they butted heads like every other family. The cheery walls around her witnessed several spirited showdowns.

That said, her appreciation deepened with maturity. When she hit thirty-four, she realized he wasn't the old man she deemed him to be when they came to him. He had a booming career and could've aimed for any number of the prospects she still had on her vision board. Two young kids disrupted all of that, and his lack of experience with children gave him every reason to refuse the responsibility. Instead, he accepted the undertaking and threw all that he had into it.

Closing her eyes, she resolved not to let Harley convince her that she put an undeserved mantel on Uncle Reed. At the same time, she realized she needed to cultivate a balanced mentality, acknowledging his limitations and the assistance he required because of them.

She awoke refreshed the next morning, but that didn't negate her need for coffee. Chewing on a granola bar, she glared at the bare space where the coffee machine used to sit and strategized a recovery mission. Back during their adolescence, Uncle Reed emphasized that they could replace possessions but not each other. Thus, they ought to invest their efforts into restoring peace rather than property, whether it was damaged or *misplaced*, as Harley frequently alleged. Being a grown woman, Lorelei recognized she could buy a simple machine for under twenty bucks, less if she took a chance on a used one. She didn't need a lavish product and only bought it to reward her uncle for decades of hard work. Why stoop to juvenile behavior she was admonished to avoid?

Because her brother still acted like a child. Why

couldn't she?

She drove out of town en route to Harley's cattle farm, her mischievous brain brewing an assortment of schemes. She didn't want to set a bad example for her niece and two nephews or make a ruckus around Genevieve. Her sister-in-law tended to get nervous without much provocation, particularly during pregnancy, and as much as this issue irritated Lorelei, she wouldn't want to cause harm to the baby. With the paranoid mother-to-be in mind, her battle plan took shape.

When she parked in front of Harley and Genevieve's farmhouse, she did a quick search on her phone to refresh her memory on a recent news item. She reacquainted herself with the facts, and grinning, she trotted up the sidewalk.

The couple never established an open-door policy with her, so she knocked. Genevieve answered it, greeting her with a smile. She embraced Lorelei as she stepped inside, her growing belly between them.

"Hey there, Lolo."

Lorelei used to grimace over the title Genevieve told the kids to call her, but the sound of the little voices saying it endeared her to it. "Hello, Mama. Congratulations on your new addition."

Genevieve touched her bump. "It's crazy, isn't it? Here, I was worried the prospect of motherhood passed me by before I met Harley, and now, we have a house full."

"Harley didn't say if you learned the gender yet?"

"We aren't going to. Everything about this has been a surprise, so we figured we'd ride that wave the whole way. I just cared about knowing how many are in there, and the doc's assured us she only sees one."

Lorelei giggled, accustomed to the line from each of her sister-in-law's pregnancies. Multiple babies ran in her family, so the subject always arose. Plus, her history in breeding dogs heightened her awareness of having more arrivals than expected.

Genevieve led her toward the kitchen, hollering to the tikes that Lolo was there. The oldest boy and girl, six-year-old Brody and four-year-old Rylan, skipped over, accompanied by the family's Pomeranian, Sprinkles. Meanwhile, two-year-old Felix peered from his highchair. She hugged the two, petted the dog, and pecked Felix's head, before she sat down at the table. Harley fed Felix across from her, a mug of fresh coffee at hand. She concealed her impish smirk, with her gaze sliding to her uncle's machine on the countertop.

"Is old Hank running all right?" he asked of Uncle Reed's SUV. Their uncle named every vehicle he owned.

"Yep. I held my breath when I turned the ignition, but it purred like always. I didn't expect it to have much gas, but the tank was full. Thank you for topping it off."

He nodded and gave her a mere *sure*, but she didn't reckon he played any part in it. If he did, wouldn't he have checked on its performance? Regardless, she chose to give him credit to promote goodwill ahead of her plot.

"How was Uncle Reed last night?" Harley asked.

"Pretty well. Gabe was there, too, so they bounced off of each other, like always."

He smiled. "Yeah, they keep the olden days alive when they're together. Did his speech hold up the whole time?"

"It did." She almost stuck with that, not elaborating any further, but her conscience beckoned her to be transparent. "He seemed to experience an episode where he sort of amped out for a second, but I couldn't make out if it was a true neurological incident or just a case of fatigue. It happened after we'd visited for quite a while."

"Well, now you realize why we've been concerned."

She perceived his satisfaction, even catching a hint of smugness in his expression. Perturbed by it, she seized the opportunity to initiate her purpose for stopping over.

She pivoted toward the coffee maker for a moment, before she pretended to do a double-take. "That's not the coffee machine I bought for Uncle Reed, is it?"

Her brother stammered. "Uh, so long as he isn't home to use it, I figured—"

"Man, you guys are fortunate that thing hasn't caught on fire! I told him to quit using it months ago. The manufacturer issued a recall on it because they're prone to overheat," she stated a true account…but withheld the fact that she later discovered Uncle Reed's model wasn't included in the scandal. "I still have the order confirmation, so I planned to exchange it the next time I came. I'm surprised he didn't convey that when you asked for it."

Yet again, she set an honesty trap for him, and she savored the opportunity to observe him try to escape it. No doubt to his gratitude, his wife rescued him.

Genevieve clutched her stomach, her mouth agape. "Oh my, babe. I kept telling you I didn't like how it sounded while it brewed. Just think of what could've happened. Thanks so much for letting us know, Lolo."

Lorelei restrained the laughter that burned within her. "You're welcome."

A glower unfurled over Harley's face. "I've never noticed it feeling unusually hot in all the time we've had it."

"As I always say, it only takes once," Genevieve replied, living up to her sister-in-law's expectations.

Lorelei rose and sauntered in the machine's direction. "I'll take care of it so you can rest easy." *And I can wake up easy.*

Harley trailed behind her and washed out Felix's dish of oatmeal while she unplugged the maker. "You'll bring the new one here, right?"

She shrugged. "I think I'll run it by Uncle Reed to see if he minds me holding onto it during my stay."

With her maniacal hysterics promising to burst free, she zipped her purchase out to the driveway and unleashed the pent-up fit there. She had to regain her composure the instant a sports convertible parked behind her, and she assumed the visitor to be a client of Genevieve's. Sure enough, a woman in designer sunglasses strode out with her miniature Poodle, ready for a fresh grooming. The lady didn't acknowledge Lorelei, even as her pooch sniffed Lorelei's legs. She followed the pair up to the house, and unlike her, the customer didn't extend the courtesy of a knock but simply waltzed inside.

Genevieve introduced the woman, Bernice, to Lorelei, and Bernice extended a cordial handshake. The Poodle stole the attention after that, and Genevieve corralled them into her home salon Harley made for her off the kitchen. He didn't want to get into the breeding business on top of growing a family, but they compromised on a grooming shop to fill her need for canines. Lorelei doubted it raked in as much as breeding, but from the looks of Bernice's posh car and apparel, she surmised her sister-in-law made enough to swing for her own upscale coffee maker.

Bernice headed on her way before long to allow Genevieve to primp her pet, and with the rest of the family commencing their Saturday routine, Lorelei departed, too. While she said her goodbyes, her gaze landed on the air-fryer, and she weighed out how she might wiggle it free. In the end, she surrendered the cause, figuring Harley deserved something for making sure Uncle Reed had a stocked snack cabinet. Plus, she didn't want to risk exposing her method with the coffee machine.

Instead of returning home right away, she made another trip to the nursing home. Her uncle didn't manifest any alarming symptoms, his mind sharp about the past and present alike. His speech never wavered, either, and he prattled about Gabe without hinting to their odd exchange the previous evening.

After a while, he grasped his phone beside him and placed his glasses on his nose. "I received a confusing text from your brother that you might be able to explain. I gather you paid him and his petting zoo a visit?"

She giggled. "I even saw the animals."

He snickered. "For whatever reason, he wanted to make sure I knew he reminded you about the recall on the coffee maker. I'll admit I can't remember things like I used to, but didn't you tell me it was fine to keep using it, after all?"

Lorelei rolled her eyes over Harley's tactics. "The machine somehow snuck off to his house, so in my state of caffeine depravation, I pulled a little sand dollar trick of my own. Mine didn't involve a dove, but I implied it was a fire hazard."

Uncle Reed shook his head. "How did you two get

such a manipulative streak in you? Don't tell me it came from me."

"Admittedly, my bit today succeeded more because of Genevieve's phobias than my cunning."

He grinned, and they shared a few minutes of chitchat, until a nurse's aide arrived to usher him to lunch. Lorelei made her way out and grabbed a bite on the ride home. After she finished off her favorite hometown burger, she devoted her efforts to another project. Given the cooler weather forecasted for Sedona, she cleaned and inspected the fireplace to the best of her ability. She was no professional, but she wanted more than anything to ensure nothing found refuge in the chimney that would cause harm or a foul stench.

Also in preparation for the cold snap, she searched for her warmer quilt, the one cherished possession missing from her room. Her mom made the pastel blanket for her, starting it while pregnant and not completing it until Lorelei grew out of her crib. She asked Uncle Reed about its whereabouts, but his memory failed him in that area. She hoped he stashed it away someplace safe, rather than the alternative possibility that her brother snatched it for one of his kids.

She did a second sweep of her closet before scouring through the others on the main floor. When none of them presented it, she tried the attic, where her sentimental uncle stored a lot of the family's keepsakes. She started her quest in the boxes that held select belongings of her mom and dad's. On countless occasions, she lingered in the photo albums, trinkets, and the sparse collection of clothes her grandma gave them after settling the estate. With dust covering them and the order of their contents the same as she left them, however, he clearly didn't disturb them.

She checked some of the other boxes, such as the ones where he secured her old toys, but they, too, appeared untouched. Running out of options, she gave up on the meaningful spots, many of which would be hard for the older man to access. She reverted to practicality, treading back to the alcove beside the stairs. The area didn't harbor many boxes but primarily stowed old furniture he should've just hauled away.

Lorelei noticed a blue tweed suitcase she never remembered Uncle Reed using, and despite her doubts, she knelt down for a gander. The fabric on it didn't show dust like the other surfaces, but its stale odor indicated its lack of use. Her logical brain needled her for even bothering to unzip the case, but she proceeded. Right before she opened the lid all the way, she caught a glimpse of her blanket on a rocking chair behind a nearby desk, but a glance into the suitcase commandeered her interest.

The canister lying in the shadows netted her attention first, as she guessed it to be from the sixties or seventies. Meticulous Reed Carmichael kept track of his unused rolls so as not to waste any, and she wondered why he missed this one. Fetching it, she spied the envelope in the opposite corner and picked it up, too. She extracted the photos inside and flipped through the stack. Frame after frame captured devastated houses, roads, and landmarks, along with a splattering of majestic mountains, lakes, and glaciers. One featured a wooden sign that was split in two but still bore the name *Chenega Village*.

All at once, she understood Gabe's statement about Uncle Reed being a resource for the story of the Alaska earthquake: he witnessed it first-hand. But how?

And why wouldn't he disclose that to her?

****

Lorelei tossed her quilt into the clothes washer, including it with a load she needed to do anyway. Five minutes after she pressed the start button, she questioned whether or not she poured the detergent into the dispenser. Her preoccupation put her on autopilot as she performed the task. She circled back to the laundry room and noted the bottle on top of the dryer, the cap beside it, and a whiff of her hand confirmed she had doled it out.

Once she screwed the cap on, she meandered into the kitchen and stared some more at the pictures and canister sitting on the counter. If she would've discovered them yesterday, she wouldn't have thought twice about developing the film in her uncle's darkroom to take them all for him to review and discuss. Throughout her entire life, he enjoyed sharing his new and old work with her and always paired it with a story of his adventures. Those conversations—which spanned anywhere between ten minutes and three hours—bred her desire to follow in his footsteps into photojournalism.

She made this revelation today, however, not even twenty-four hours after Gabe's veiled comment about Alaska and Uncle Reed's elusive reaction. Though she continued to debate if his condition played a part in his behavior, Gabe's apology led her to believe Uncle Reed manifested an emotional reflex as opposed to a random incident. Now that she uncovered proof of his connection to the Alaska earthquake, her conviction of it solidified. His omission of this trip and reluctance to divulge anything about it even now were no accident.

Reasoning that it would do no harm, she opened her

laptop and researched the earthquake. In all honesty, she'd only ever heard of the fact that a big one happened there and didn't give it much consideration. If she were to work up a piece about it, she'd need to research it, anyhow. Besides, it'd pacify her curiosity...or so she thought.

She studied the statistics, namely that it still held the record as the most powerful quake in North America and killed over one-hundred people. While it impacted the whole state and areas as far as Seattle, Washington, the disaster leveled several towns, including Chenega. The pictures from the suitcase attested to that. The more she read, the harder it became for her to believe her uncle didn't utter a word about his experience there.

The detail that fascinated her most was the date, March twenty-seventh, 1964, just months before her parents' death. The photos didn't feature a timestamp, but comparing them to the images on the web, she observed Uncle Reed's didn't feature snow on the ground like the ones online did. The difference led her to conclude he took his later in the spring or summer, closer yet to her and Harley's arrival. She vaguely remembered her grandma telling them they couldn't fly to Sedona until Uncle Reed returned from investigating a story. Could this have been his subject?

She accessed the Mountainscape News website, the journal where he worked, and ran a search through their archives for any article pertaining to the earthquake. Another writer composed the lone report about it two days after it struck. For good measure, she put the topic and his name through a general search engine in case he sold it to another source, but nothing materialized. Considering the fifty years that elapsed since then, she took into account that his piece may not have been digitized, or the outlet could've folded long before the Internet became popular.

Scrutinizing the undeveloped roll next to her, though, Lorelei couldn't shake the notion that the story he planned to tell grew into something more.

****

Lorelei tucked away the film and photos into her uncle's desk in an attempt to reestablish the boundary between them. Just as she resented Harley's disregard for Uncle Reed's belongings, she didn't want to overstep and take advantage of the circumstances, either. The somber truth occurred to her that they would have to comb through his possessions someday, but she wouldn't take that liberty until forced to.

For the next few days, she continued to settle in and visit Uncle Reed. During every chat, she mulled over his condition and how they correlated with his living arrangements. She had yet to discern any troubling red flags with his mental state, but upon joining him in a physical therapy session, she became more aware of his lack of mobility. The strong man who used to hike in the mountains and replace cracked tiles on the roof now struggled to cross a small room without holding onto rails. She maintained a supportive spirit as she sat beside him, but she let her tears slip out once inside the car.

That evening, she determined to convince Harley they needed to get him discharged. His routine in the facility didn't permit him to exercise like he could at home, and she anticipated he'd recover better under such conditions. She would stay with him as long as he couldn't manage alone.

Reality intervened, however, before she had the

chance. Wednesday morning, her feet froze when she entered the room and beheld him limp in his wheelchair, eyes glazed and mouth open. Panicked, she hollered for help, and her legs rallied up the strength to carry her toward him. The quiet breath expelling from his lips sent hope surging through her, and she rubbed his arms and shoulders to rouse him out of the stupor. No matter what she said or how she patted him, the haze didn't lift.

When the nurse strode in, she tried speaking to him while she checked his pulse. She also stuck an oxygen monitor on his finger.

She shifted toward Lorelei. "His pulse is elevated, and his oxygen's on the low end. Your brother probably told you we've gone through spells like this before."

Lorelei nodded. "I didn't realize they were this severe."

The nurse studied him for a few moments. "He usually gives some sort of response. I think we'd better send him to the hospital for observation."

Lorelei agreed to the plan, stroking his back as she fought back tears. She accompanied him in the ambulance and called Harley after they wheeled Uncle Reed into the emergency department. She expected an arrogant retort from her brother, but he expressed his sorrow and told her he'd rush over.

After she hung up the phone, she approached the receptionists' desk and inquired if she could be with Uncle Reed. The woman contacted the staff inside the department, then instructed her how to locate the holding room where he was. Navigating through the corridors, she spotted him in a cubicle that had its curtain partially drawn open. He sat upright on the bed, bright-eyed, appearing like a completely different man than the unresponsive one with whom she rode there.

When she glided through the entry, he regarded her with the same startled look she leveled at him. "Lorelei? How did you get here so quick? Weren't you in New York?"

She buried her dismay. "I was a week ago, but I've been home to spend time with you."

He nodded in acknowledgement, but she couldn't read if he remembered. She suppressed the urge to question him, not wanting to upset him. Deep down, she dreaded how he might answer.

He scanned his surroundings. "Did they change my room?"

She dragged the adjacent chair closer to the bed and sank down. "No, this is the emergency room. You gave me a scare back at the home. You kind of…blanked out for a while."

"Are you telling me that nephew of mine is right?"

Despite her heartache, she laughed. "I'm as appalled as you are by it."

He smiled and offered his hand, which she held on top of the blanket spread over him. His eyes conveyed their angst, crippling her to the core. It evoked memories of the rare storms that hit Sedona and how he always kept his calm demeanor. On the one occasion he displayed his worry over the possibility of landslides, her own stomach churned with nerves.

The doctor who was attending to him, Dr. Marx, stopped in and evaluated Uncle Reed, while Lorelei scrutinized his every expression. He asked the patient a slew of questions to test his cognition, which Uncle Reed passed apart from the date and current president. After that, Dr. Marx interviewed her about the incident at the home. Because of her protective instinct, she grappled with providing honest responses, as she never liked to frame her uncle in a bad light. At the same time, logic reminded her that something was wrong, and the best chance to get him the needed care was to admit it.

Even so, she tensed up when Harley joined them at the tail end of the consultation where Dr. Marx had requested his perspective. Surprising his sister, he didn't bombard the doctor with bleak claims. Instead, he offered matter-of-fact statements regarding Uncle Reed's declining balance and the mental glitches he witnessed. He related that none of the episodes lasted as long as this one, nor did they seem this critical.

Dr. Marx jotted down some notes and wrapped up the discussion. "This could be a fluke or a byproduct of your low oxygen level, but since this is progressing into a recurrent issue, I'd like to run a couple of tests. That way, we can determine whether or not these occurrences are pointing to a more serious condition."

"Like what?" Uncle Reed asked without delay.

"I don't like to speculate, sir—"

"I worked in journalism for eons, Doctor, and people sandbagged me nonstop about matters that, I'll confess, weren't always my business. When it concerns my vitality, however, I demand straightforwardness."

Lorelei recognized a glimmer of amusement in Dr. Marx's eyes before he replied, "There's a condition called akinesia, which are periodic stints where people lose all function of their muscles and faculties. Medications are available to help minimize the frequency of the episodes. Unfortunately, it's linked to several diseases."

"Like what?" Harley echoed his uncle.

Dr. Marx sighed. "I'm afraid the most common is Parkinson's."

****

Lorelei staggered into the house, numb from the day's events. She slung her purse onto the kitchen table and hunted for sweets to fill the void growing deeper inside of her by the minute. When Uncle Reed's favorite snack cupboard greeted her with bare shelves, disappointment crashed into her and not just because of her unsatisfied craving. Rather, like everything else during the previous nine hours, the empty cabinet demonstrated that nothing stayed the same forever.

Following suit with her few past encounters with the emergency room, most of their time consisted of waiting. They had to wait to get into the tests Dr. Marx ordered, before waiting some more while they ran them, just to wait for the results. In actuality, they were still waiting, given that they had yet to learn the results, but the doctor put a temporary hold on their suspense by admitting Uncle Reed for the night. Through it all, Uncle Reed didn't suffer any more episodes.

The MRI and blood tests they performed enabled them to rule out a stroke and a heart attack. Neither report eased her mind, as her worries spiraled around the prospect of Parkinson's disease from the moment Dr. Marx declared it. The editor-in-chief at the first journal she worked at in Phoenix was diagnosed with the disease not long after he hired her, and his symptoms progressed quite rapidly. She didn't work there much longer than two years, and he resigned months before due to his regression.

She unearthed a candy bar from the drawer that stored the potholders and an occasional goodie. When she and Harley were kids, their uncle used it for his secret stash, figuring they wouldn't bother to peer inside. They proved his theory right for several years, until Lorelei began baking for her school's fund-raisers. Even after she caught onto his scheme, she respected the border line and never revealed it to her brother, whom she gathered, prompted Uncle Reed to continue employing the hideaway.

She munched on the snack, which still delighted her taste buds despite its being on the stale side. Meanwhile, she contemplated the numerous scenarios that swirled around her brain all day. She refrained from hopping online to dive into the worldwide web of self-diagnoses, having swam into those endless and fearsome waters during past medical scares. Once she took a few bites of her treat, the constant drone of potential calamities faded, especially when her gaze latched back onto the drawer where she placed the photos and film.

In light of the ordeal that morning, her uncertainty over Uncle Reed's reaction to Gabe's remark about Alaska grew. What if he had just lost control for a brief moment, and the topic of conversation didn't play any factor in it at all? On the other hand, he concealed both his trip and the evidence of it for her whole life with him. Dare she cross that long-established boundary and dig into his property, which he clearly guarded? Shouldn't she bow to his right for privacy, like she did with his hidden sweets?

She dismissed her nagging curiosity again and padded into the living room to catch up on some emails and phone calls. She gave Gabe a heads-up about Uncle Reed being in the hospital earlier in the afternoon, but she updated him on what transpired since then. The question she longed to ask him burned inside her mouth, but she swallowed it. Before its bitter aftertaste subsided, a message from Calvin Thompson appeared in her inbox with the subject line, *Alaska or Bust?* She groaned in exasperation and dimmed the screen, not needing to read the email to discern what it concerned.

A force propelled her back into the kitchen. Even in the moment, she couldn't define whether it was weariness, a yearning for a preoccupation, or desperation to cling to something that drew her closer to her uncle. Whatever the case, she pulled the drawer open and nabbed the canister. Without paying heed to the ethical qualms that pecked her conscience, she retreated to Uncle Reed's home darkroom.

Chapter Three

Lorelei twisted the knob of her favorite room in the house, struck by warm nostalgia once again. Even before she could operate a camera, she relished each opportunity to study her uncle's beloved task. Many times, his photographs' subjects didn't matter to her…but that wasn't the case on this occasion.

She couldn't estimate how long it'd been since he used it, given the fact that he begrudgingly switched to digital during his final years with the paper. True to her predictions, the supplies cabinet contained all she needed to process the film he never did. Certain he would've used 120 medium format film, she prepped the correct reel and mixed the solutions. After that, she switched off the main light.

The first time Lorelei developed film with Uncle Reed, he instilled in her not to concentrate on what each image featured but to focus on the tints and sharpness. That way, one wouldn't get too distracted and sacrifice the quality to produce the optimum photographs. When he instructed her as a nine-year-old, she didn't have a clue how to detach herself, too interested in her snapshots of their trip to the zoo back then. With age, she acquired the technique, and she sometimes became so absorbed in the process that she almost forgot what batch she was working on until she finished.

This bunch, however, challenged her skills, starting

with the test strip. Without a spare negative lying around, she had to use one of the frames on the roll. She hated to waste any of the twelve images, considering her oblivion over what they displayed. She held the magnifier up to her eye and inspected just a couple to decide which to choose, before selecting a mountain landscape similar to one in the envelope. She placed it under the enlarger and slid a sheet of photo paper beneath it, freezing it for five-second intervals, to determine the ideal exposure time.

With that out of the way, she moved on to the rest of the roll, viewing them through the enlarger one by one. The first few portrayed more of the devastation, with one showing a lone schoolhouse standing amidst the rubble. She recalled a website she visited in her research that mentioned the school being the only building in Chenega to survive the quake. In the next frame, residents began to show up, many of them surrounded by the homes they lost. One in particular tugged at her heartstrings, as an indigenous woman stared at the debris with her little boy leaning against her pregnant belly as he clutched a little stuffed animal.

While she proceeded dipping the pictures into the developing solutions, her thoughts wandered around the reasons Uncle Reed didn't discuss the adventure. In his years of covering stories, he'd witnessed various tragedies, including several wildfires, but nothing this profound in loss. She could only imagine how the prevailing sorrow affected the sensitive man. With it occurring just before her mom and dad died, his despair over everything he beheld would've been compounded by the grief their family endured. Perhaps he always associated the two events together.

Having just three negatives to go, she peered at the

next rendering through the enlarger and recognized the same little boy but without his mother. With a campfire in the background behind him, he wore a smile, and although it didn't showcase her uncle's artistic talent like the rest, it conveyed a powerful message about a child's resilience. His mom joined him again in front of the fire, her face brightened with more joy, as well. Lorelei surmised Uncle Reed befriended them, but she didn't ascribe much value to it until she secured the final shot under the enlarger.

Projected onto the wall above her, the boy and his expectant mother beamed back at her, with her uncle beside them. Even at first glance, she perceived his adoration, his countenance brimming with the same pride and gentleness he had in many of their family photos. The longer she studied it, though, the more signs she gleaned of this being a man in love.

Entranced by it, she snatched the paper below it away, not wanting to chance ruining the print of the beautiful scene. Her gaze traversed the portrait inch by inch, mesmerized by the side of her uncle she'd never been privy to in her lifetime with him. After she assimilated the tenderness radiating from his eyes, she noticed that he had one arm wrapped around the woman's waist, with the other hand resting on the boy's shoulder. Neither of the adults tilted their faces toward each other in the cheesy prom-like pose common to new couples, but the trio appeared comfortable being in close proximity.

Before long, her intrigue shifted from the precious sight to the identities of those living it. By all counts, the man mirrored Uncle Reed's physical characteristics from the era, with his sandy sideburns extending the length of his ears and his nose similar to her dad's. Though he grinned much like he did with her and Harley beside him, he stood with a different stature, manifesting a confidence foreign to her. She didn't consider him an insecure man by any means, but this version of him shined with an air of belonging.

As for the mother and son, on the other hand, she couldn't place them whatsoever. Her speculations about their relation to Uncle Reed bounced around in her head and toyed with her emotions. The woman's stomach—protruding more here than in the first photo—kept hooking Lorelei's scrutiny. Her well-mannered, professional uncle wouldn't stand this way with another man's lady. If he were taking it for a story, he'd want to present them as a family, wouldn't he?

Unless they were the family.

Lorelei adjusted the dials on the enlarger to zoom in, not caring if it blurred for the moment. On instinct, she focused on the boy first, searching for familiar features. She didn't find any distinctive resemblances, with his face being a different shape altogether. Of course, his ethnicity gave him darker skin and hair than her uncle, so she couldn't base much off of those factors. Still, he didn't have the traits that dominated the family line, such as the nose her dad, uncle, and brother shared and the pronounced forehead hereditary to the Carmichaels, including her. Nonetheless, her brow rose when her enhancement highlighted Uncle Reed's fingers encompassing the side of the woman's belly.

Genetics could do funny things, making a child a clone of one parent without much likeness to the other. While she couldn't draw a dogmatic conclusion on that aspect of the matter, she knew her uncle and father-figure well enough to be sure he would never abandon his own children. He had every chance to desert her and Harley, kids he'd only met on a handful of occasions up to the day they were orphaned. Instead of pressuring her aged grandparents to take them or letting them go into the system, he welcomed them in and provided the love and stability they so needed. The notion he'd do that after leaving little ones he fathered defied logic and ran counter to the guy who raised her.

Lorelei emerged from her trance and processed the film at last. Just the same, she scoured the image again and again for clues into this mystery as she immersed it in the solutions. The final step, the fixer bath, solidified it onto the paper, reviving the moment to life. She hung it up to dry with the rest of the pictures and examined the end-product, Uncle Reed in particular. Inside, she burst with a mix of love, perplexity, and a bit of somberness over the fact that whatever this encapsulated didn't continue.

****

Lorelei packed a tote full of snacks the next morning, expecting to spend most of the day at the hospital. Sure enough, she arrived just after eight, and by twelve, they still had yet to talk to a physician or hear of any further tests that would be run. She refrained from eating the munchies in front of Uncle Reed, uncertain of his restrictions before whatever procedures the day might hold in store. When they offered him the lunch menu, the nurse informed her that none of the scans they may do would require fasting. Once he gulped down the roast beef, spinach, and cheesecake—all of which he accused of being overdone—she handed him a snack cake she bought at a gas station along the way.

Finally, Dr. Waverly, the neurologist, moseyed through the door, and after exchanging formalities, he provided good news. Having examined the MRI results, he detected no signs of Parkinson's but wanted to perform a PET scan before he made a conclusive diagnosis. Of course, he didn't rush him to the diagnostics wing and related that it may take a few hours more for them to fit him into the busy schedule.

With no plans for the immediate future, Lorelei obeyed her uncle's request to go for some lunch. Per his recommendation, she skipped out on the cafeteria and drove across the street for a chicken sandwich. By the time she returned to his room, Uncle Reed slept in the bed. At first, she worried he was having another akinesia episode, but his closed eyes and relaxed posture indicated it to be a normal nap.

As she gazed at him in his slumber, she caught glimpses of his younger self. Though the wrinkles creased his soft skin, his chiseled jawline still stood out and gave him a distinguished appearance, while his almond-shaped eyes exuded his warm nature. Until she pondered it, she never considered when this or that changed as far as his appearance was concerned; the evolution of his abilities and stamina seized her attention more. After seeing the photo of him in Alaska, she could better identify the similarities and differences between the two versions of him. She teetered between embracing and resenting them. She bubbled with pride over her uncle's growth and accomplishments through the decades, but like the grains of sand in an hourglass, the signs of age enhanced time's irreversible march.

Beyond that, her discovery made her muse about who he might've been if he'd stayed with the woman and

44

her son. Uncle Reed didn't apprise them to any dates or girlfriends during their childhood, but later, she assumed he must've snuck out once in a while. He worked overtime now and then, telling them he had to finish up a story, so she grew to figure he fibbed in order to maintain a social life. He never displayed loneliness, either, which contributed to her contentment not to clamor for a husband. In light of this, however, she lost her certainty in the conclusion that he just led the life of an average bachelor…with two kids in his house. Had he hidden an endless love for the woman all these years?

A tap on the open door thrust her out of her reflection, and Gabe waved in silence. She motioned for him to sit in the chair beside her. They spoke a couple of whispered sentences, before Uncle Reed awoke.

Uncle Reed smirked at his friend. "Are you here to update the obituary they keep on file at the office?"

"Nah, nothing much has changed since you became a retired old fart!"

They broke into chuckles like always, and Lorelei appreciated the refreshment of their typical banter, complete with the references to bodily functions. Somewhat to her surprise, Gabe didn't concentrate on Uncle Reed's health, but he acted like he would under any circumstance. She gathered that, being in his elder years, too, Gabe understood the toll it took to have to regale everyone with the same details over and over. She chimed in here and there, but she let them take the lead and enjoy their time together.

Within twenty minutes, a nurse interrupted them, arriving to take Uncle Reed to the long-awaited PET scan. She loaded him into his wheelchair, and the guys exchanged goodbyes. Gabe and Lorelei remained seated, with him using their moment alone to voice the curiosities he muzzled around his friend.

"Any idea what this test is supposed to uncover?"

"The neurologist said he's inclined to rule out Parkinson's, but he wanted these results before he made the call. I haven't decided if that relieves me or adds to my worry."

"From my experience with Clara, I learned the only thing worse than not knowing is knowing."

She squeezed his hand in support, remembering his wife's years-long battle with skin cancer. Lorelei hadn't been in town often through that time, but Uncle Reed kept her attune to the developments of her fight. It started with a dermatologist having to remove an occasional area of concern, which didn't trouble them a whole lot because of how routine the procedure was. When a patch appeared on her back, the dermatologist referred them to an oncologist, beginning a series of treatments. Her condition improved and worsened in spurts, until the disease metastasized and claimed her life four years ago.

After letting a silent spell pass between them, Lorelei tried to brighten the mood. "How are the grandkids?"

"Draining my bank account with all their milestones. We were ecstatic when the girls ended up pregnant around the same time, but it didn't take us long to realize the costliness of it. They get their driver's licenses together, graduate together, move out together, and get married together. I'm sure the trend will continue and carry on to a new generation. Meanwhile, Grandpa's supposed to be there with his wallet. Clara used to harp on about not spoiling them, but the way I see it, they insist on not getting the same gift unless it's cash. I'd rather slip a bill in a card than run around trying to find separate presents that are sure to be returned all said and done."

She laughed. "Considering the pace at which Harley keeps reproducing, I think I'll follow in your footsteps."

He winked and stood up, and she escorted him out of the room, welcoming the chance to stretch her muscles. En route to the elevator, he told her, "By the way, Olive wanted me to convey her apologies for not swinging by since you arrived. With Candace being a senior, she's been busy traveling to basketball games and scouting colleges. I can't believe how busy this generation keeps their folks."

"Understood. I guess it's a good thing I never had kids. I can barely keep up with my own agenda. I'll text her and try to hammer out a day when we can catch up."

A man and woman exited the elevator as Lorelei and Gabe neared it, so Lorelei hustled to reach it before the doors closed. Succeeding, she held it open for him and punched the button for the lobby. In the empty cabin, her thoughts veered back to the subject of Alaska. Her mouth remained locked, until her curious mind and desperation fused together to form the key.

"Global Expeditions is badgering me for an answer about my ability to go to Alaska. I can't make a decision until we figure out Uncle Reed's prognosis."

Gabe murmured an acknowledgement but offered no input.

She understood the response to be a sign of his reluctance to say any more, but she couldn't forfeit her mission. "Didn't you mention something about Uncle Reed having insight into the Alaska earthquake? He had a little glitch that didn't allow you to elaborate."

Karina Bartow

His neck expanded because of his hard swallow. "He did some research on it when it happened, that's all."

"For a story?"

"Yes. It was a big headline, being the most powerful quake to strike the country. Plus, Alaska became a state just a few years prior to that, so everyone took even greater notice."

"I'll have to read his article. How can I access it?"

He paused while they strolled across the lobby. Once outside, he shrugged. "The article didn't make it to print. His hard-nosed editor wouldn't give him enough space on the page to do the story justice, in his opinion."

She giggled at his reference to himself in the third person and nudged him in jest. The remark served as a playful way to divert the conversation, and she obliged him when he switched topics to the weather. She ushered him to his car and almost let him off the hook, but before he could duck behind the wheel, her hand plunged into her purse. She extracted the picture she'd concealed all day.

She displayed it to him. "Uncle Reed went to Alaska, didn't he?"

He offered a meek nod.

"Who are the woman and boy?"

"I never had the opportunity to meet them."

"But you know who they are, don't you?"

Gabe dropped his gaze and tilted his head toward the building. "It's not my story to tell, sweetheart."

Regret pinching her, she nodded. Gabe bent and settled into the driver's seat while Lorelei waved. Right as she pivoted on her heel to retreat inside, he lowered the passenger's side window. She approached it.

"Do your uncle a favor," he said, "don't address this

48

with him. He doesn't need it on top of everything else."

With guilt piling up inside her, she drummed her fingertip on the inside of the car door, a habit she fell into as a child when she was in trouble. After a beat, she expressed an epiphany she'd just made. "I'm sorry for being so forward and sticking my nose in his business. During the past few months, I've been fixated on…all of the unknowns ahead. Since I heard your comment and came across this, I'm faced with different unknowns, but they concern the past. I just want some answers if they're out there and maybe shed some new light on my uncle."

He didn't give an immediate reply but twisted the ignition key. Before pulling away, he stated, "Everybody has parts of their lives they want to keep hidden in the shadows."

****

Lorelei's insides coiled up within her, feeling like they were pasted together in a bundle in her stomach for the rest of the afternoon. Between Uncle Reed's medical crisis and her exchange with Gabe, every thought that materialized in her brain evoked misery and uncertainty. The lack of distractions in the sterile room compounded her unrest, so she flipped on the television while Uncle Reed remained in testing.

Once the nurse wheeled him back, her uncle put on a good show, making jokes about being poked and prodded. His demeanor grew more serious, however, after another nurse reported that the neurologist would stop in later with his results. He didn't eat much of the dinner they served him, and while he blamed it on the poor quality of the food, his refusal of even the chocolate pudding indicated more lay behind it. Lorelei opted to have the untouched dessert, but her nerves robbed her of the pleasure in it, too.

Their anxious anticipation appeared useless when the sun set and darkness enveloped Sedona, but the nurse maintained Dr. Waverly would make it over. Just after seven, the physician—who Lorelei guessed to be at least fifteen years her junior—waltzed through the door. His smile disconcerted her, as she wondered if he plastered it on when he had bad news to share.

After they exchanged salutations, he displayed his tablet to them, which featured one of Uncle Reed's brain scans. He referred to it and circled several areas during his discourse, but the visual aid didn't mean much to Lorelei's untrained eye. "The images we took gave us a pretty good idea of what you're experiencing. This rules out Parkinson's disease, like I suspected, and you're also clear of any tumors. What I do notice are some abnormalities in the frontal lobe, particularly in the areas that affect balance, which explains your recent falls. On top of that, these deposits have formed on your tissues, which can be a marker of Alzheimer's disease."

Lorelei swallowed hard when he uttered the name.

"In your case, though, I don't see any other indications of that. We don't have past scans with which to compare these, but your brainstem shows signs of atrophy. If you study this part in the midbrain closely, you might make out this bird shape. It's called the hummingbird sign. A few different conditions are associated with it, but everything considered, my colleagues and I agree we're looking at progressive supranuclear palsy. It's a rare condition that targets men, especially, over sixty, and its symptoms are consistent with yours."

The mouthful rendered Uncle Reed speechless for a

moment, before he posed the obvious question, "What's the prognosis?"

"We don't have a cure, but we can give you medication to suppress the symptoms. The ones on the market increase your dopamine levels, which helps with movement control."

"By definition, it is progressive, right?" Lorelei asked.

Dr. Waverly nodded. "Patients do get to the point of needing round-the-clock care."

Ever the sharp-shooter, Uncle Reed questioned, "How long do I have?"

"On average, people live five to seven years after diagnosis. Given that you're not complaining of trouble with your eye movement, another primary signal, I'd say we caught it early."

Uncle Reed gave a shrug. "Five to seven years is about what I hoped for, anyhow."

Lorelei and the doctor chuckled over his bluntness, before Dr. Waverly continued, "An outlook like yours helps a lot. With you already being in assisted living, you won't undergo much of a transition, either. Overall, you're in good shape."

That's a funny phrase to say in the context of a terminal diagnosis, Lorelei thought. She understood what he meant and admitted that, in the grand scheme of things, everyone was dying. She also appreciated Uncle Reed's point about accepting five more years, at worst. At eighty-four, he'd outlived some of his closest friends. Even before this incident, she sensed his time dwindling away, which prompted her to venture home in the first place.

Having a title and timetable attached to his mental

state, however, enhanced the imminence of it. Not only would he succumb to this someday, but he'd have to suffer through the regression of the illness. Sure, age alone wreaked havoc on one's abilities, as she was beginning to learn all too well, but realizing its link to this invisible enemy compounded the frustration.

Dr. Waverly jarred her out of her contemplation when he asked if she had any follow-up questions. After she said no, he strode out of the room. She locked gazes with her uncle and mustered a grin, unable to determine what reaction he'd like from her. Because of his easygoing response, she didn't want to deflate his good spirits, but at the same time, she hated to convey that the news didn't devastate her. For that unsettling moment, she figured skydivers with defective parachutes leveled that same cockeyed smirk at each other.

"After Gabe hears about this, he's bound to start calling me 'bird brain'!"

Lorelei faked a giggle but then grew serious. "We should get a second opinion, considering the rarity of this."

Uncle Reed shook his head and waved the notion aside. "Honey, it doesn't matter the term they give this. Dementia, Alzheimer's, Parkinson's—who cares? My body's just breaking down, and there's no reversing it. Life is a one-way street with an ultimate dead-end, and I'm thankful mine has extended these many miles. If I get five to seven years more, that's enough to construct another rest stop."

She laughed for real this time. "I'm sure you'll put in a new bakery or two. Speaking of rest, I reckon we both need some, so I'll head out."

She leaned down to give him a peck on his cheek,

and he gripped her hand. "Now, just because my road is nearing its end doesn't mean yours has to. I appreciate you came back to try to spite your brother, but as much as I hate to admit it, I suppose he did the right thing. You still have a lot to do to make me proud while I'm here. You don't need to stand by and watch me lose my mind."

She snorted and tucked her hands into her pockets. "Thank you for saying that, but you have no room to talk. You redirected the entire course of your life for us, and the more time that passes, the deeper I understand how selfless that was. Carmichaels don't abandon each other; we recalibrate."

Uncle Reed's eyes twinkled with affection as he winked.

****

On her way home, tears trickled down Lorelei's cheeks while she processed the day's discovery. Her mind commanded her not to blow this up but to adopt her uncle's viewpoint about his long life. She remembered when he hit sixty—a much older milestone twenty-five years ago than she deemed it today—and her fear that it'd be his last decade. He made it two more since then, and she should embrace that. Given her parents' sudden and young deaths, how could she overlook the gift of his longevity and even the opportunity to prepare for life without him?

All the same, her heart needed the chance to mourn, and from her past experience in therapy, she realized she shouldn't resist that. Her pain ran deeper than the prospect of her losing him, with her most bothered by the threat of him suffering. Despite his and the doctor's remarks about the nursing facility suiting his needs best, she despised the thought of him undergoing these significant changes in a bare and foreign room. He needed to be in the home he established when he was twenty-six and where he nurtured the family he didn't plan to have.

And maybe had always imagined sharing it with the one he intended to make.

Lorelei batted away the quandary of the woman and little boy the instant their images popped into her thoughts. She had weightier concerns to tend to. Still, the matter snuck up on her now and then throughout the evening, as she hated for Uncle Reed to lose his memory of them if he cherished them the way she suspected he did. She debated whether or not she should show him the photo and see how it developed from there, but she also worried the emotions would worsen his condition.

Shelving the dilemma, she meandered into the house, and while she settled in for the night, she mulled over the measures it would take to accommodate his limitations. Being a ranch-style home, it would permit him to navigate pretty well in his wheelchair as long as he had assistance. They'd need to swap out the bathtub for a shower stall, but she didn't foresee many other major adjustments they'd have to complete. Her biggest challenge would be having someone to care for him during her workday.

She researched home care options on her laptop, until an email notification distracted her. The message came from Calvin, declaring it to be his last call for her to take the Alaska story. She read it, along with the one she didn't open yesterday. He bumped up his offer again, and in light of her ideas to provide suitable living arrangements for Uncle Reed, she couldn't ignore all it could do to further the cause. Now that they clarified his prognosis, she could afford a short trip without the imminent threat of his demise…or so she hoped.

Thus, she replied to the editor and accepted his proposal. At the very least, it'd boost her finances so she could honor her uncle like she wanted to. At the very best, she'd have the opportunity to uncover a glimpse of how the place shaped him.

Chapter Four

With almost two weeks before she had to depart for Anchorage, Lorelei stayed mum for a spell about her project and what she intended to do with her earnings. She didn't want to appear apathetic to Harley's plight and selfish enough to bug out at this critical juncture. On the flip side, she resisted inciting him to poke holes in her initiative before she could prove she had the means to execute it.

The following days didn't test her resolve very much, as she continued in the pattern she maintained since her arrival. She made daily treks to the hospital until Uncle Reed was discharged Saturday afternoon, then resumed her journeys to the nursing center. Meanwhile, she investigated different services he'd qualify for once he was at home and what his insurance would cover. Her need for Harley's authorization as his healthcare proxy thwarted a few of her efforts, but she managed to compose a general outline of how they could move forward.

As she compiled those notes, she also expanded her search into the Alaska quake so she could have a battle plan for her travels. Calvin sent her several old photos he had permission to use that he wanted her to restage to highlight the changes of the landscape. In truth, she preferred Uncle Reed's shots, particularly the one with the mother and child peering at the vestiges of their home. In view of the fact that Uncle Reed didn't know she'd discovered them, however, she couldn't ask for his consent, nor would she take the liberty of featuring them without it.

During her quest, her intrigue rose more and more over the subject of Chenega. The island, located in Prince William Sound in the Gulf of Alaska, lost twenty-six of its sixty-eight residents in the course of the earthquake and the tsunami that followed it, with the village never being fully rebuilt due to the crippling damage. Survivors sought refuge elsewhere until the community resettled on Evans Island in 1984. Their hardships didn't end there, with an oil spill occurring on the coast five years after that, ironically on the twenty-fifth anniversary of the quake. The calamity rocked their subsistent culture, robbing them of their fishing industry and harming their wildlife.

Again, Lorelei yearned to discuss all of this with her uncle and learn the boy and woman's story. She wondered if they kept in contact and whether or not they set up a home on Evans Island. In the decades that elapsed, did they flee Alaska altogether? Were they still alive? Many questions about these people, whom she couldn't even name, swirled around her head, but one beckoned loudest: What did they mean to her uncle?

She had to accept the distinct possibility that she may never find out. She still added Evans Island and Chenega as potential stops on her short adventure, but a consultation of her map app gave her pause. The areas would entail more than a day's voyage unless she flew by helicopter.

She didn't fret over making it work but figured she'd leave her options open. As her departure approached, the need to declare her itinerary to the guys daunted her more. She fessed up to Harley first in an effort to see if he could chauffeur her to the airport. While he agreed, his expression showed the smugness she expected, like he anticipated her to dash out of there sooner or later. She fought the ire bubbling inside her, still not ready to confide her goals for Uncle Reed in her brother.

Lorelei put off telling Uncle Reed about her job until the day before her flight, afraid of how the topic might affect him. She regretted her procrastination in the end, with Gabe present when she planned to break the news. She continued to delay it, hoping Gabe would take off before her, but since she had some packing to do, she couldn't stay for very long.

Pressure built within her as she confronted the issue. "I took a project that will keep me away for the rest of the week, but I'll be home next Wednesday. It's quick money."

"Don't you love those?" Uncle Reed beamed, not appearing to connect the dots from their conversation at the nursing home. "What does it concern?"

She treaded with caution. "It's the one from Global Expeditions."

Her words met with a wince from Gabe, who offered a brief nod and peered over with downcast eyes. Uncle Reed, on the contrary, didn't manifest any recognition.

His eventual reply proved his bemusement. "I guess I missed that tidbit. What kind of piece did they request?"

She sneaked a peek Gabe's way, noting the elevation of his raised, bushy eyebrows. "A reflective piece, one about how communities have recovered from disasters."

"Sadly, we have far too much material to use for that subject," Uncle Reed replied. "What's your destination?"

To her gratitude, Gabe swooped in to assist. "They probably need you to hop around to several spots, don't they?"

She bobbed her head but reeled in her desperation. "Yeah, I'll be running around a few locales. Like you said, we're not lacking for content."

He accepted the response without further inquiries, which came as a relief to her. Any other day, she would've stressed over her uncle's lack of recollection of a matter she mentioned not that long ago, but in this case, she'd take it. She still debated whether he was experiencing symptoms of the supranuclear palsy, given what they'd learned about his heath since then. Considering her revelations about his love life, she wouldn't dare chance it.

They wrapped up their visit, with the men wishing her safe travels. Uncle Reed kissed her hand when she stood to leave. While she and Gabe hugged, she perceived his desire to say something, but his lips remained closed. Instead of leaving the building at the same time as her like usual, he sat back down. She hoped he didn't hold her choice to go against her.

She couldn't focus on what he did or didn't think, having to complete her dash for suitable attire for the artic trip. Given she'd flown from her apartment in Charleston, she didn't bring more than a couple of light sweaters and a spring jacket to Sedona, very unprepared for winter weather. The forecast now showed lower temperatures than it predicted earlier in the week, with highs grazing twenty degrees Fahrenheit and lows dipping into the single digits. Thus, she made a last-minute decision to buy a pair of insulated boots and down parka.

Moments after she finished stuffing her suitcase Thursday morning, Olive, Gabe's daughter, appeared on her doorstep. Truth be told, she would've rather not had an unexpected guest, seeing as her scheduled flight would be taking off in less than four hours. Nonetheless, she managed to smile when she greeted her friend.

"Dad told me you're about to head out, so I won't stay long. I just wanted to swing by when I could. Dad's kept me posted with the latest on your uncle. I'm so sorry for all you're going through."

After their embrace, Lorelei replied, "You've been in pretty much the same boat."

Olive sighed. "Something's bound to catch us at one point or another, but for some strange reason, we're never prepared to discover what it's going to be."

"Nope. I keep contrasting it with what happened to my parents and the agony of them being gone without warning. I can't say I prefer that to this, but the possibilities of how it'll play out can smother you. I'm most afraid of losing him little by little as his mind goes."

"I understand. During Mom's last week, she faded in and out of consciousness and didn't recognize us for the majority of her wakeful moments. That killed our family more than any of the other parts of her decline." She squeezed Lorelei's hand when she extended it. "I'm glad you're getting away, even if it is business-related. Have you ever traveled to Alaska?"

"I've hit parts of Canada, but nothing has arisen like this. I'm looking forward to it."

"I've always wanted to go, too. Stan and I may go

on a cruise there to celebrate our twenty-fifth. It will depend on how good of a scholarship Candace gets," she said. "Well, have a marvelous trip. Dad wanted me to pass on this reading material. He says he couldn't justify bringing it on his own, but he wasn't opposed to sending it by courier. Hopefully you understand what that means better than I do."

Lorelei took the manila envelope. "I think I do. Please convey my deepest gratitude."

Olive assured her that she would and wished her a safe flight. Once alone, Lorelei ached to tear out the contents of the package, but she couldn't spare the time. She fought her impulses and remembered she'd have six hours in the air to devote to it. She secured it in the front pocket of her carry-on bag for easy access and started to close it, before another compulsion struck her. Rushing into her bedroom, she drew out the batch of photos her uncle took. A part of her worried about losing them along her journey, but she resolved to keep close watch on them. She doubted they'd be of use to her professionally, but she couldn't resist having them to pair with whatever Gabe's reading material would reveal.

The doorknob clicked from across the living room, making her stash them on top of the envelope and zip the pocket shut in a hurry. She hoped her face wasn't flushed from her panic, but she didn't figure her oblivious brother would even notice. Sure enough, he gave no heed to her appearance, with his gaze darting right over to the kitchen counter.

"How's the new coffee maker brewing?"

Prepared for this from the instant she snagged it out of his house, she gave a simple response. "Strong, just how I like it."

She did a final check of her purse to ensure she had everything but regretted taking the precaution when it allowed Harley the chance to wander over to the machine. He scoped it out, and before long, he said, "This was our old one. I recognize this scratch from when Brody ran his toy truck up and down it a few months ago. Did you fabricate that recall bit altogether?"

She raised a brow. "Did you ever ask Uncle Reed's permission to take it in the first place?"

He stammered, until he reverted to his selfish ways. "If neither of you are going to be here to use it this week, can't I take it back? With Genevieve pregnant and not drinking any, it's a hassle making a whole pot just for me. She doesn't like me to waste it, either, so I'm reduced to sipping on the old stuff for two days."

"Sounds like you have two choices: Either enjoy a few extra cups or use better birth control!" Her remark made him shake his head, and she laughed. "Okay, you can keep it warm for me until I get home. I suppose you deserve it for driving me all the way to Phoenix. Try putting some toothpaste on a sponge and scrubbing it on that scratch so she doesn't notice that it's the same one. That worked on a stainless-steel fridge I had."

"I'll give it a shot. Thanks."

As he unplugged it and cradled it like an infant, aggravation crept back into her throat. "I'd appreciate you returning it when I come home. Otherwise, I'll have to tip your wife off to the dangers associated with air-fryers."

He sneered. "Very funny."

The mood remained light during their two-hour journey south. They no longer had anything to debate about Uncle Reed's care, with Harley exonerated by

Uncle Reed's diagnosis. He hadn't gloated—at least not out loud—but on the occasions they spoke about him, she detected pride in his voice as he hailed the nursing home's *wonderful* care. Because of that, she swerved the conversation away from the subject.

He tested her determination when he surprised her by fishing for her long-term plans. "When you mentioned this being home back at Uncle Reed's, does that mean you're going to stay put after this?"

"Sedona's always been home, no matter what. I haven't put down roots anywhere else in my whole adult life." She almost concluded her explanation there, but her conscience goaded her to continue, "In all honesty, though, I think I will stick around here more. According to Gabe, I have a standing invitation at Mountainscape News, and I'm inclined to take it for a change. Uncle Reed showed up when we needed him most, and I couldn't forgive myself if I deserted him at this crossroads just to satisfy my ego. This job in Alaska caught me off-guard, and I would've refused it if the pay wasn't so great."

He nodded, appearing to accept her reasoning. When he cleared his throat, she wondered if any of her words pierced him with guilt, but none of her remarks stemmed from animosity—on this occasion, at least. Rather, she voiced her own feelings, as the past several weeks had altered her view of both her past decisions and future ones.

She reflected on her younger days, when she chose to make photojournalism her profession. Uncle Reed burst with pride, and although he allowed her free reign to decide where to work, she always sensed his yearning for her to end up at Mountainscape. She humored him and Gabe by taking an internship there in college, which netted her the first byline of her career. Aside from that, she didn't hesitate to break out of her uncle's shadow, despite her deep love for him. While he bred that passion for photography in her and taught her everything she knew, the independence common to young adults made her buck at following his path so implicitly.

She didn't regret her entire career, and Uncle Reed's sweet comments in the hospital about making him proud assured her of his admiration. Still, remorse pricked her over some of those times when she downgraded Mountainscape, if only in her mind. She gave her younger self a pass, since most kids itched to carve their own mold, but she despised the way she handled things when he retired and prodded her to take his position. She declined with grace, but she doubted she'd managed to conceal her opinion that it'd be a demotion for her. In retrospect, she understood his wish for her to carry on his legacy there, as well as the opportunity it would've afforded them to be together through his later years.

She pumped the brakes on falling into a pit of self-reproach and redirected her focus to the adventure ahead.

"I'm sorry I couldn't take off from Flagstaff. All of their flights had multiple and long layovers, so it would've taken twenty-four hours to get up there."

He shrugged. "I don't mind once in a while. I come down here to get our hay for the horses, so I'm going to take advantage of the chance to buy a load on my way home."

"I appreciate it. I could've parked in a garage for the duration, but I worry about theft. Then again, I'm not sure a bulky, thirty-year-old SUV would attract somebody."

"A catalytic converter grabs attention, no matter what."

Lorelei welcomed the unusual ease that accompanied their back-and-forth, and it prompted her to disclose more than she expected to. "I didn't admit that I'm headed to Alaska to Uncle Reed. Gabe recently told me that he went there to write a story about the earthquake right after it happened, so I didn't want to trigger any bad memories from it. Since he never mentioned the experience to me, I'm uncertain of how it affected him. From the pictures I've seen, I can imagine the profound level of tragedy."

Harley downplayed her assessment. "Uncle Reed witnessed a lot in his career, and none of it seemed to faze him. That said, I don't remember him saying anything about Alaska, either. Considering we could never persuade him to take us on a snow trip, maybe it did do a number on him."

In all her hours of musing, that connection hadn't occurred to her, and she agreed with his observation. She let out a genuine snicker, recalling the way they begged him every winter to go experience the snow in the mountains up north. She didn't give it a whole lot of thought, besides her disappointment whenever he said no, but now, his stalwartness intrigued her. He usually seized the chance to take them places, no doubt to satisfy his own travel bug, so why not accommodate them just once? Did he really hate the cold that much, or did snowy environments conjure up the memories he strived to suppress?

After she didn't reply, Harley promised her, "I won't tell him where you are."

She thanked him, and within fifteen minutes, they

entered the departure loop at the airport. She prepared to grab her luggage and purse once they reached her airline's kiosk. She and Harley didn't share much of a farewell ritual, so since she only packed a carry-on, he didn't even get out from behind the wheel. With a line of incoming traffic following him, he gave her a simple goodbye before he merged back onto the byway.

She commenced her typical trek through the airport, enjoying the added perk of avoiding the long security line thanks to her new enrollment on the TSA pre-check registry. Her expediency granted her an extra twenty minutes to roam, but this time, she zipped right to the terminal instead of browsing through the stores. As much as she delighted in exploring the unique products the shops sometimes offered, the envelope from Gabe captivated her more.

She made one detour to the donut counter, grabbing a chocolate-frosted long john to nibble on while she read. She sat down with it in a secluded corner and drew the package out of her bag. Peeking inside, she spotted several smaller envelopes along with some letter-sized papers clipped together. When she slid the pages out, she noticed an index card attached. It reminded her of the notes Gabe usually left on Uncle Reed's drafted articles, but this one had her name on top.

Lorelei,

I've debated sharing these with you for weeks. Reed barred me from discussing this long ago, but my Clara made me save the article and notes in case he ever changed his mind. I hope the insight they provide will give you some solace and help shape your piece.

The message induced a smile to cross her lips, as she had no trouble envisioning Clara, a hopeless romantic, urging her husband to preserve the mementos. A part of Lorelei burned with desperation to start with the notes, but since she already had the article in her hand, she poured over it.

On March 27, 1964, people across Alaska shuddered in terror at the alarming sound that echoed through the air. Some residents feared an atom bomb had detonated, while others suspected a plane crash. The moments thereafter proved it to be a nine-point-two magnitude earthquake, which forever changed Alaska's coastline and the lives of its people.

Nobody fared as badly as the natives of Chenega Island, located on the state's southern tip. Of the 131 victims who perished in the tragedy, the Chenega tribe lost twenty-six of their members, constituting one-third of their population. With the village of Chenega sitting on the Prince William Sound, many were fishing to provide for their families when the quake struck and may have assumed they were safe after the initial shaking stopped. The tsunami that followed, however, showed no mercy, despite their profound reverence for nature.

A core value of the Chenega people is embodied in the word Unguwacirpet, which means "Our way of living" in the Alutiiq language. The term encompasses their acknowledgement of their lives being sustained by the natural world, which they don't take for granted. On the contrary, they cultivate a deep respect for all the resources they depend on, which shapes how they hunt and fish. Thus, this calamity that destroyed their home came as the ultimate betrayal.

The powerful introduction ushered in a compelling narrative that demonstrated yet another side of Uncle Reed that Lorelei hadn't beheld before. She always admired her uncle's journalism skills but believed his talents in photography outweighed them. In this, though, his humanity shined through his writing style, propelling it to new heights. He stuck slide-sized copies of his pictures to the draft, but his words gave life to his depiction that even images didn't capture. As she studied the article, she realized he wasn't just composing this for Mountainscape News; this would've landed him a piece in a major journal and more than likely an award or two.

After giving his observations, he quoted a variety of survivors. Along with them, he provided descriptions of the scars some still bore as well as their expressions while they spoke. His empathy for their plight framed the remarks, despite his professional approach. Supporting his earlier comments about the tribe's commitment to nature, a couple of elders expressed remorse over allowing the land to be regulated by the federal government now that Alaska was adopted by the States. Before this, they oversaw how everything was handled, and they made clear their belief that this was the cost of their lack of control. While she didn't share their conviction of the earthquake being nature's retribution against them, she admired their dedication to the environment.

Lorelei became so caught up in the riveting account that she almost forgot about her original subject of interest. Uncle Reed's next eyewitness reminded her of it.

Nadua Macawi was preparing acorn bread as a special treat for her family to celebrate their new addition, a second child expected in the fall.

"When I felt the first trembles and heard that deafening clap, my priority was to protect my children,

my son seated in his highchair and the one developing inside of me. I had no concept of what was going on, but my instinct beckoned me to get low. I grabbed my son and retreated under our table. The house crumbled around us. I didn't expect to survive."

After the ground settled, Nadua traversed her demolished home with her toddler son in tow. She met up with her brother-in-law next door, in search of her husband, Matto. The brothers fished together that day, but Matto stayed out longer. They set out to find him, but the incoming tsunami forced them to seek shelter, instead. Three days later, Nadua succumbed to the fact that her husband and the father of her children wouldn't return home.

As she gazes at the rubble where her kitchen stood on that tragic evening, she strokes her little boy's hair with one hand and her stomach with the other. Heartache over the past and worry over her future without Matto are etched in her eyes.

"Matto built this house for our family, and he's gone, along with his gift to our children. I'm lost, but I know he'd want me to carry on for them."

Lorelei dabbed at a tear. Uncle Reed didn't attach the photo of the woman and child, but she could envision them in the moment he described. Given the tender shot was on the undeveloped roll, she wondered if he intended to include it or if he'd already decided to keep it just for him.

The rest of the article, though well-written, didn't provide any more revelations, and Lorelei's mind hovered around the reference to Nadua. Her emotions teetered between sympathy for the woman and an odd sense of relief Lorelei didn't anticipate. Ever since she beheld the photo of her uncle with the mother and child, she rejected the very traces of the notion of Uncle Reed deserting his own family. Just the same, the context this offered dispelled the reservation that lingered inside her.

After she finished, she shuffled the pages back to their proper order and tucked them into the envelope. She started to fish out one of the notes, but a text from Calvin interrupted her. By the time she sent her reply, the waiting area stirred with the first boarding group about to cross the terminal bridge. She figured she'd better resist her impulses and zip up her bag to ensure she didn't lose anything during the jaunt to the plane.

Peering around the gate, she marveled at the number of passengers that crowded the place. Throughout her decades of traveling, it never ceased to amaze her how many people headed to the same destination, regardless of the season or tourism appeal. When she departed from Arizona in the winter, she usually assumed most were trekking home, and this group's demeanor made her surmise the same. With an older couple being a few seats away, she debated asking them if they experienced the earthquake, but she didn't want to offend them with her forwardness.

She pivoted the other way and noticed a camera on the floor a few feet away. Given it resembled hers, she did a double-take, afraid it'd spilled out of her case. She quickly determined it was a different brand, before she realized a man wore a case on his shoulder.

"Excuse me, sir." Lorelei pointed to it when the man raised his head. "Did that fall out of your bag?"

He glanced downward before bending over to retrieve it. "Yes, it is. I must not have zipped it up well enough after I passed through security. Thanks very much."

"Sure. They're none too cheap these days."

She studied his camera with interest. While the model didn't appear to have as many bells and whistles as hers, it differed from the simple point-and-shoot kind most people traveled with, if they even still owned an actual one. He had a detachable lens on it, and she caught sight of another one with higher magnification in his satchel. "Are you a professional?"

He shrugged. "My daughter would tell you I am, but I don't really claim to be. It's been a hobby since I was a kid, and now that I'm retired, I've accepted some freelance work. I don't have a studio, but friends of mine commission me for weddings and so forth." He hesitated before extracting a business card from his pocket. He smiled as he handed it to her. "My daughter printed these up for me."

"Nice to meet you, Mack Holt. I'm Lorelei Carmichael." She handed him her card and examined his closer. She recognized the listed phone number's area code as one from Alaska. "You must have quite the following to be requested all the way down here."

"Nah, this was a personal trip. My daughter and her husband just welcomed their first child, so they wanted Apaa to take his first photos."

Lorelei had to conceal her astonishment over the man being a grandfather. Not a strand of gray tainted his jet-black hair, and his olive skin remained smooth without even the crow's feet that were threatening to grace her temples. She didn't guess him to be much older than herself, but then again, she supposed—with a gulp of trepidation—she could've been a grandmother or close to it if she'd taken the traditional family route.

"I'm sure Apaa was happy to oblige." She grinned, as Mack nodded with his smile widening. "Would you mind my asking what language that is?"

"Alutiiq, our tribal family's. Her husband is from the Apache tribe here, but when I agreed to let them marry, I made them promise to keep our heritage alive in their children." He assessed her card. "You're a photojournalist? Would I recognize any of your work?"

"It depends on what you follow. I've been published occasionally by Global Expeditions. I'm on assignment for them right now, in fact. They're doing a story on the fiftieth anniversary of the earthquake."

A somber cast dimmed his brown eyes, but he didn't address the subject. "I don't read many periodicals, but that's impressive."

She thanked him, right as the ticketing attendant announced that the rest of the passengers needed to line up according to their designated boarding zone. Lorelei congratulated Mack on his grandson, but the parting words proved to be unnecessary when the two ended up in the same line. Accustomed to airport etiquette, she normally would've left their conversation at the seats and reverted to the role of stranger, but a question popped into her mind that she couldn't repress.

"From what part of Alaska does your tribe reside?"

"The southern coast. A lot of them live on Evans Island."

The instant he uttered the name, Lorelei understood why his tribal family sounded familiar; she'd run across it in her research and just read it in Uncle Reed's article. The people of Chenega were part of the Alutiiq tribe. They moved to Evans Island after the earthquake demolished Chenega, which meant Mack's family was likely among the survivors.

Chapter Five

Lorelei forged onward to the eighth row of the plane where her seat was located and hoisted her carry-on into the overhead bin. In an effort not to delay anyone behind her, she'd slipped out the envelope Gabe gifted her while she followed the travelers who weren't as adept at organizing their belongings as she was. She carried it to her window seat and stashed it in the pocket attached to the seat ahead of hers for safekeeping until after takeoff. She realized the space wasn't the cleanest, but having to fly as much as she did, she disregarded the germs long ago for the sake of her sanity.

Her gaze shifted toward Mack, but she didn't let it linger so as to give him the wrong impression or make him uncomfortable. While she couldn't deny her attraction to his dark features and the warmth that he emitted, her fascination primarily centered on his possible ties to the earthquake. Given his younger appearance, she couldn't discern if he would've been fifty yet and had lived through it himself, but the journalist in her wished she could learn his family's perspective. His downcast expression indicated he had a story, but his failure to volunteer it made her back off, even if it ran contrary to her training.

She willed him to sit down beside her, but he continued on toward the rows behind her. He grinned over as he passed, but she refrained from craning her head around to observe how far he trekked. She accepted that the extent of their interaction was probably through, similar to her exchanges with countless others she crossed paths with throughout the years. On this occasion, however, she didn't believe he would dwarf into a nameless, barely recognizable figure after she exited the airport.

Because of how she planned to spend the six-hour flight, she hoped her seatmates didn't care to make much conversation. During her decades of journeying, she'd run the gambit on companions, with some talking themselves breathless in ten hours and others not uttering a syllable. To her gratitude, a newlywed couple joined her, on their way home from their honeymoon, and aside from greeting her, they seemed unaware of her presence for the duration. Their incessant canoodling and endless expressions of affection would've normally rankled on her nerves, but in this instance, she just put up her own imaginary curtain.

Once the aircraft soared into the cloudless sky, Lorelei retrieved the envelope and extracted the stack of notes. Gabe's age and absence from the newsroom did nothing to diminish his meticulous organization skills, as he placed them in chronological order, indicated by the dates in the corner. Upon beginning the earliest one on top, her uncle's familiar writing style and terminology again cloaked her in both security and eager expectation.

Gabe,

I meant to write you before this, but I had difficulty getting settled. Nothing prepared me for the war zone, by all appearances, that I've entered. Roads still lay ripped up right through the middle, power lines scatter the ground, and once-thriving businesses stand dilapidated, if they even stand at all.

As I relate this, guilt pierces me, considering how much worse these poor locals have it, with their lives utterly devastated. Reading the fact that 131 victims perished is tragic, but the stale statistic doesn't begin to capture the true toll on these people. The number doesn't encompass the loved ones left behind, whose dreams and very foundations of their lives have been shattered.

This was impressed upon me on my second day here, when I visited a school cafeteria that has been converted into a shelter for the displaced. I interviewed as many of them as possible. Though the accounts of the quake itself mirrored one another, the stories they shared of the aftermath varied in such heartbreaking ways. I can't fathom any photos I snap or words I compose being able to translate the magnitude of impact on these people.

The instant I strode through the door, my gaze inexplicably darted right to a beautiful indigenous woman who was caring for her toddler son. I spoke to several others before I made my way to her, and while I endeavored to give them my utmost attention, I couldn't keep my eyes from sliding in her direction. Sure, her striking yet natural loveliness attracted me, but her demeanor captured me most of all. Even from afar, I perceived her sadness, but her countenance as she tended to her little boy showed her underlying strength.

When I introduced myself at last, she manifested reluctance to open up to me. Normally, I would've moved along, but I decided to ask the young boy about the homemade stuffed moose in his hand. He told me it belonged to his "taataq", his term for his father, and from his mother's tears, I surmised that they'd lost him. Before she opened her lips to say anything, her fingers stroked the small bulge of her stomach that carried another child, explaining the added agony in her plight.

I didn't pry, but the woman, Nadua, divulged her experience of being in her home on the island of Chenega when the quake hit. She awaited her husband to celebrate their new addition, but he didn't make it back to her, killed by the tsunami as he concluded his day of fishing. She expects her baby to be born in three months, without her husband, a home, or a livelihood.

In that moment, this became more than a career-boosting story for me. A part of me is ashamed to use these tumultuous events for personal gain. Some have admonished me, though, that they appreciate having their travails documented in order that others recognize their pain. I've heard many more in Chenega suffered losses like Nadua, and I intend to learn as many of them as I can. I'd like it if she'd assist me in doing so, but I wouldn't want to heap any more of a burden on somebody who's loaded down enough.

Another mix of emotions swirled through Lorelei over her uncle's narrative about Nadua. Relief spritzed her yet again due to the answers it gave to the questions she'd contemplated in the past few weeks. At the same time, however, a sorrow accompanied it. She wished Uncle Reed had shared this piece of his life, as his affection for the woman was evident from this first encounter.

Folding it differently from the others in order to keep track of the ones she read, her heart warmed with appreciation for Uncle Reed's profound empathy. While there were occasions—especially during her teen years—when she accused him of not understanding her, she almost always found a compassionate audience with him. He had a natural way of relating to her when she'd share her struggles. Being a girl without a mom to confide in, she cherished the effort he made to guide her with a steady yet sympathetic hand.

His sentiments about the death-toll tugged at her heartstrings, too, with it reminding her of similar admonishment he used to give her and Harley. Whenever they'd learn or in her case, report on a calamity that inflicted casualties, he'd correct them for downplaying it if the number wasn't very high. He pointed out the fact that their lives were upended by a fire that *only* claimed two lives, those of their parents. The lesson stuck with her, and from the note, she realized he'd probably learned it from the earthquake, months prior to her family's tragedy.

Before she slipped out another note, a flight attendant made her way to Lorelei and the newlyweds' row with her cart of drinks. The couple chose canned cocktails to extend their celebration, while Lorelei opted for a simple soda like usual. Once she took her first sip and munched on the accompanying pretzels, she proceeded with her reading. The next two letters weren't very effusive like the opening one, as Uncle Reed mentioned Nadua's name just once. With it confirming she and some of her neighbors had agreed to go along with him to Chenega, she anticipated the follow-up to contain more. The photos of her and her son in the rubble that used to be their home revealed what an emotional day it must've been.

Sure enough, her uncle's dark yet kind tone attested to the intense experience.

Gabe,
We just returned from Chenega, the journey having

taken five days. We traveled by boat to the island, which made for such a bitter-sweet environment among these survivors. As we rode over the waves, surrounded by the blue waters glistening under the sun, peace prevailed, especially through a tribe of people so embedded with nature. At the same time, this very water caused much of their heartache and is the final resting place of many of their loved ones.

Words fail me with regard to describing how inspired I am by these people. They wore their sorrow, so much so that I regretted suggesting we make the trip. The majority expressed that conditions were worse than they remembered when they fled, being too traumatized by it all to absorb it back then. I conveyed my guilt, but each of them assured me that the venture provided them closure and courage to sally forth.

As for Nadua, I couldn't read her for a lot of the day since she and Makya, her little boy, remained so quiet. I sensed her attempts to stay strong for him while they toured the site where their house stood. Afterward, I stumbled upon her breaking down once her brother-in-law took Makya for a walk. I did my best to comfort her, but I wouldn't deem my efforts adequate.

In the end, she, too, believed the return helped her in facing hers and her kids' future. With the past unsalvageable, she's more inclined to pursue a fresh start. Between you and me, I'm beginning to wish that fresh start could include me.

I've enclosed a draft of the introduction to my article.

The draft wasn't included this time, no doubt mailed back to him by Gabe with some notes and edits that enhanced it to the version she already examined. Still, she doubted it was any too rough, given the letter's tone matched his later writing so closely. The next note confirmed her assumption, opening with a grateful acknowledgement of his boss's input. It also implied Gabe had mentioned Clara being entertained by the love story unfolding, as Uncle Reed teasingly suggested buying her a romance novel so she could get her fix from that, instead.

Lorelei glanced at her watch and discerned they still had more than three hours before they'd touch down in Anchorage. She'd made a substantial dent in the stack of letters and could probably finish them well ahead of their final descent, but she needed a break. As much as she savored getting acquainted with this new aspect of her uncle's life, the various responses it evoked in her heart sapped her of energy.

Deep down, she understood that her parents' death and his decision to take them on had been what ripped him away from Nadua. The few references he made to her disclosed his growing affection for her, and Lorelei figured the remainder of the notes would reinforce that even further. The child in her reared her cowardly head, being afraid to uncover the one that said he'd lost the love of his life because his brother's kids needed a guardian. Given how quickly he must've flown home after the fire, the adult in her reckoned that conversation probably occurred in person, but she resisted just the same.

Uncle Reed's brief remarks about Nadua made her real to Lorelei. Despite the decades that had passed since he penned them, she couldn't keep from envisioning her as the young pregnant mother he described and photographed. His depiction of her troubles tore through

Lorelei and made her just as remorseful about depriving Nadua of love as she was for her uncle. This woman already experienced tremendous loss, and perhaps just when she began to embrace a glimmer of hope in Uncle Reed, he slipped through her fingers, too.

Gazing out the window at the dark sky, the clouds around them just slightly illuminated by the plane's headlights, she contemplated whether she'd follow her uncle's example if the need arose. Would she have enough love for her family to sacrifice the life she wanted? Truth be told, Uncle Reed hadn't interacted with her and Harley before the fire any more than she did her own nieces and nephews to this day. Almost every time Harley and Genevieve asked her to babysit while she visited, she weaseled her way out of it, resisting the notion of being taken advantage of during her vacations. Given their rapid reproduction rate, they didn't seem to need extra date nights in her opinion.

She realized those circumstances were different, but this new insight into Uncle Reed's pursuits before they changed his priorities made her even more grateful. Up to now, she rationalized that he took them in because he didn't have any other obligations that tied him down. Discovering he had Nadua and Makya, with whom he may have been better acquainted than he was her and Harley, showed her the depth of his dedication to her parents and them.

Guilt pierced her, as she couldn't deny the selfish tendencies she displayed throughout her life. No matter how she attempted to justify her choices, she had to admit, if only to herself, that she wouldn't have altered her world in the drastic way her uncle did for her.

Rather than dwell on the regret over her past,

however, Lorelei resolved to channel it into motivation to be more generous from this point forward. She reaffirmed her drive to take care of Uncle Reed after she returned from Alaska. In the meantime, she hoped that the place her uncle once cherished could somehow lead her to help him revive the memories he deserted in that undeveloped film while he still could.

****

Lorelei opened her sleepy eyes as the pilot announced that they were making their final descent into Anchorage. She hadn't intended to nod off for the last ninety minutes of the flight, but she considered it for the best, given the local time was two hours behind Arizona's. Plus, she had much settling in ahead of her, checking into her hotel and all. She still breezed through the process, but her energy definitely waned quicker now that she'd surpassed fifty than when she was in her thirties.

She didn't regain her full alertness until she peered out the window and marveled at the glorious Aurora Borealis dancing amidst the stars. In her few jaunts to Canada, she always seemed to miss the phenomenon, whether it be the wrong time of year or weather conditions. Here, though, the view was completely unobstructed in the clear sky, above the reach of the city lights awaiting them. For one of the first times she could remember, the spectacle captivated her on such a profound level that she didn't scramble for her camera, not wanting to live it through a viewfinder. Nonetheless, she prepared a mental checklist of the lens and filter she would utilize to capture the blue, green and pink hues when they appeared in the nights ahead.

Never one to create congestion during the hectic

arrival shuffle, Lorelei stayed put and permitted the most frantic passengers to shuffle through the cabin first. She kept her focus outside, where the Northern Lights maintained their brilliance despite the illuminated surroundings. In the distance, she could make out silhouettes of glaciers across the waters of the Cook Inlet, which reflected the celestial wonders overhead. She'd landed on many a runway through the years, but this one fascinated her more than any of them, notwithstanding the late hour.

After the initial rush of fleeing travelers subsided, she rose to her feet, maintaining a firm hold on the envelope of letters. Her infatuated seatmates already departed the row, so she moseyed closer to the aisle. While she debated when to merge in, she took a gander toward the back of the plane and spotted Mack in a similar stance but talking on the phone, no doubt with his family. She endeavored not to stare, the same way she had during the entire journey. By her count, she gave him five glances, including when he boarded and the pair of restroom breaks they each made. She didn't catch his eye on any of those occasions, however, and doubted he cared enough about her to notice her location or movements. She couldn't explain why she paid attention to him or why disappointment pinged her that he didn't reciprocate her curiosity—much less why she tallied her peeks at him like a teenager.

Whether he intended to or not, Mack forged ahead right on time to take the position behind her in line. She almost made a remark about exiting together as they entered together, but her lips clamped shut, afraid of seeming foolish. She remained quiet in the close quarters, bidding adieu to the pilot and flight attendants when she neared the exit. In the terminal, Mack circled over to her side, making her expect him to dash past her. On the contrary, he kept in step with her.

She didn't hasten to say anything but did her best to initiate a natural conversation. "The night's sky here could keep me entertained for hours."

"The lights are stunning tonight. You tend to take them for granted when you're a local, but this is only my second time landing among them like we did."

"I've never witnessed them before, so that was quite an introduction. I was too mesmerized to grab my camera."

He took the bait she half-intentionally set. "I snapped a few shots, but I know from experience they never do it justice. Would you like to take a look?"

"Of course."

He swung around the bag that hung from a shoulder strap and powered on his camera after retrieving it. Once he set it to viewing mode, he scrolled through them in front of her.

The images impressed Lorelei, showcasing his talent for framing and getting the ideal temperature of the colors. "I'll admit there's nothing like the real thing, but those are as close to it as one can get. You've perfected it, for sure. I can only hope to get a few that can match yours."

He shrugged. "You're a pro, so I don't think you have anything to worry about. You have my card, though, if you'd like me to send them over."

"My email address is on my card, so just plan on doing that after you settle in at home. I'd love to have that memento of our welcoming committee." *And of you.*

He agreed to do so, and after toggling through the

picturesque scenes, he hesitantly offered to share more. "I claimed I wouldn't do this, but would you care to see my grandson?"

She grinned, recalling how Harley professed the same before he started a family but also caved within instants of becoming a father. "Please, go ahead."

The doting apaa presented a few of his collection, showing some of little Ahanu alone and a couple of others with his parents. "My daughter, Halyn, chose the name in hopes of instilling a good nature in him, since it means 'He laughs,' but at this point, the joke's on them. The kid has such a grumpy face! We tickled him and did all types of nonsense to prompt him to curve up his lips, but he wouldn't cooperate."

She chuckled. "With a loving apaa and parents, I'm sure he'll cheer up eventually."

Though she wasn't acquainted with his family, her brief glimpse of the photos revealed Halyn inherited her father's kind smile. She could envision Ahanu developing it as well, even if many of his features favored his dad right now.

After he finished giving her the sampling, he returned the camera to its holster, and they fell silent. She continued to expect them to part ways, especially when they neared the restrooms, but they both bypassed them and stayed in-step. Once they ventured away from the main terminals, the airport offered a variety of stuffed animals native to the state, some in display cases and others free-standing on their mounts. Unable to resist the impulse to play tourist, she took a shot or two of the polar and brown bears along with the popular moose that a family also on her flight posed beside. Her stops made her lag behind Mack, who had clearly seen them all before.

She wished he would've told her goodbye but didn't fault him for not, considering she rarely gave strangers a proper send-off while traveling. Because of the late hour and the fact that they were on the last returning flight, the small crowd didn't clutter the concourse, which permitted her to maintain a visual on him. Still, she didn't hustle back up to him or stare at him. Why would she? Even if they accompanied each other all the way to the exit, they'd separate within minutes and probably end up discarding both business cards.

Accepting the reality that their short encounter ended, another fact of life struck her, and she entered the nearest restroom. After she finished, she resumed her trek but halted her steps upon noticing the display of Anchorage's history through the decades. The placards showed aerial shots of the city and how it changed over the course of the century. Most were spaced in ten-year intervals, until 1960 gave way to 1964. Taken right after the earthquake, the photograph captured the drastic contrast created by the catastrophe. The entire landscape changed, with buildings upended and massive drop-offs in the ground where it used to lay flat.

She would've liked to have lingered by the feature wall to study it, but when a nearby night guard scrutinized her, she remembered the need to scoot so the building could close. She snapped some photos for her article as well as for future reference; she could zoom in and read the captions later.

She waved at the guard, apologetic. "I'm sorry. Just interested in the earthquake."

To her surprise, his expression softened, and he paced her way. "I can relate. I didn't move here until '87, but I've heard a lot of stories through the years. You should check out Earthquake Park. It's just a few miles away and has more information like that."

She wished she could've asked him about the accounts he'd heard, but with the clock ticking, she just thanked him for the tip.

Lorelei bypassed the baggage claim area, having only packed her carry-on, and consulted her phone to refresh her memory on which hotel Calvin booked her. She accessed the confirmation email and groaned when she read the request to call the free shuttle ahead of time to ask for a lift, with the disclaimer that it may be a twenty-minute wait. She regretted forgetting that part of her routine due to the wonder of being somewhere new, not to mention the handsome fellow she met. She almost submitted a request through her ride share app but figuring that could take the same amount of time, she gave the shuttle a try. Thankfully, the hotel clerk reported that others were staying at the same place and had already summoned them.

With the help of the clerk and directory signs posted throughout the thoroughfare, she located the vehicle. She raced toward it upon noting that the last of those waiting was almost aboard, and she had to catch her breath once she sprung up the bus's first step. Illuminated brighter than the dimmed airport, the sharp lights above shocked her pupils, making spots appear everywhere and revealing her true sleepiness. After her vision cleared, she observed similar drug-out expressions among the group, before her gaze landed on a familiar face. She secured her suitcase with the rest of the luggage stowed in the cargo bay and sat down beside grinning Mack.

"You're not following me, are you?" he teased.

"You caught me. Your daughter tipped me off about your extraordinary talent, and I'm recruiting you to be Global Expeditions' next star photographer."

He harrumphed. "I wouldn't put it past her."

Lorelei chuckled. "Are you sticking around Anchorage for a while?"

"Just for tonight. I actually parked my truck in the hotel's lot to save some money, so I figured I'd get a few winks before I head home. I'm not sure if I'll come out too far ahead financial-wise, but it beats funeral expenses if I fell asleep behind the wheel."

"Very true. My editor cut a corner by not reserving me a car until tomorrow, but with my exhaustion, I appreciate his penny-pinching."

Mack acknowledged her statement with a yawn of his own, and they rode in silence for the remainder of the drive. The shuttle stopped under the carport right in front of the entrance, and they lined up to depart. As she did on the plane, Lorelei didn't rush ahead of the crowd but waited her turn. Again, Mack displayed similar patience.

Half of the travelers strayed off to the parking lot, no doubt using it in the way Mack did, while the others continued into the building to check in. Because of her haste to catch the bus at the airport, she hadn't noticed the frigid nip in the air, but even in the thirty seconds it took to retreat into the building, she shivered in her coat. A true gentleman, Mack encouraged her to go ahead of him, so she entered the lobby and completed her business with the concierge. Her nosey side wondered if he would be given a room near hers, but her manners—and drowsiness—prevented her from loitering around to eavesdrop. Instead, she took her key card and waved goodbye to him before she navigated to the elevator to take it to the fifth floor.

With her assigned room across from the lift, she didn't need to wander the hallways in search of it. Entering it, she didn't bother to perform her usual checklist when setting up her accommodations but simply changed into her pajamas and collapsed into bed. While she lay there, the envelope of letters peeked out of the case seated on the adjacent luggage stand, awakening the discoveries she'd already made about her uncle's Alaskan adventure. She ruminated on the last one she read and his hopeful remarks about Nadua's fresh start including him.

She still cringed that the fresh start that transpired wasn't the one he had in mind. If nothing else, she determined to use what she earned on this job to grant him one more fresh start that he so deserved.

Chapter Six

Lorelei's eyelids crept open, prompted by the sliver of sunlight that peeked through the curtains she neglected to close tight. She'd always heard about the darkness that accompanied Alaskan winters, so she didn't deem it a big deal to leave it cracked. Besides, she couldn't sleep in too late, regardless of how little slumber she netted. She had less than five days to collect the visuals and testimonies she needed for the feature article which Calvin would expect to be well researched and thorough to justify her hefty payday.

That pressure barreled down even more when she retrieved her phone and read his text informing her she had to pick up her rental car by ten. Already a quarter till nine, she snapped out of bed and washed up, foregoing her typical post-travel shower until later. Once dressed, she slung her purse around her shoulder to carry it cross-body and tucked her camera inside in the event she ran across something of interest.

Her phone rang a couple of times as she proceeded with her routine, but she disregarded it. When it resounded again, her instincts compelled her to answer, especially once she realized Harley placed all three calls within twenty minutes and left her a voicemail before she woke up. Her heart thumped with fear for Uncle Reed's wellbeing.

"What's going on, Harley?"

"Did you notice if Uncle Reed had any more hazelnut coffee pods in his pantry?" her brother asked. "We're all out here."

Lorelei rolled her eyes and pinched the bridge of her nose as her head started to pound from the wave of fear that crashed into a wall of irritation. "Let me think. I remember spotting it somewhere." She paused to stir his anticipation. "Oh yeah, in the grocery store. You can have as many as you like, for a price, of course."

"Thanks, sis," he muttered. "I just figured I'd conserve what might go to waste before I buy more. Doesn't sound like your extra sleep helped your mood."

She darted across the hall to the elevator and commissioned it to transport her to the ground floor. "What extra sleep? I hardly had seven hours. Keep in mind, I'm two behind you."

"I forgot that. Guess you won't care if I give you a call at three our time, when I'm up changing Felix."

"One nighttime activity leads to another, bro, and neither is any of my business."

"Fair enough, but it shows you why I need my caffeine fix."

She gave him that much and concluded the sparring match as she paced into the lobby. The room appeared foreign to her from where she checked in eight hours earlier, now a bright expanse bustling with activity. Like the airport, it showcased the state's wildlife and culture. Skis and snowshoes hung above the concierge desk and yet another stuffed bear overlooked the seating area. Guests crowded the breakfast buffet, making Lorelei's stomach growl. With it closing at ten-thirty, she doubted she'd make it back in time to take advantage of the complimentary meal if she didn't grab a bite now.

She refused to give into her hunger, considering she didn't want to lose Calvin's reservation. She headed toward the front desk to request a shuttle back to the airport complex, where the rental company was located. She stopped when she overheard a guest locked in a dispute with the manager and clerk over charges to her room, which promised to ensue for a while. Shrugging, she veered off to the dining area in search of a baked good she could scarf down during her wait.

Before she joined the food line, Lorelei noticed Mack at a table by the fireplace that flanked the space. Once again, his presence reawakened that jittery but delightful spark she believed had remained hibernated since college. Her feet drifted a pace in his direction before she rooted them back in place. She wouldn't revert into the desperate teenage girl who used the restroom farthest away from her classroom to chance encountering her crush at his nearby locker.

It employed more self-control to resist approaching the Belgian waffle-maker, her guilty pleasure that was disappearing from many hotels. For this hurried morning, she seized a plain bagel and bottle of orange juice and began to nibble on her breakfast as she padded back to the concierge. The miserly lady's argument with the staff dragged on with her equally-cheap husband by her side, so Lorelei couldn't estimate how much longer the hold-up would continue. Another receptionist stood behind the counter, but she seemed too flabbergasted by the ordeal to proceed with her job.

At last, an assertive man entered the queue and zipped right up to the young woman, apathetic to her unpreparedness. Lorelei followed him and peered away from the confrontation just as Mack strode up to take his position behind her.

She gave way to her clever side, echoing his remark from the previous night. "You're not following me, are you?"

He grinned. "Ironically enough, I mentioned meeting you to my daughter when she checked in with me this morning, and in all honesty, she badgered me to ask you for a job."

Lorelei chuckled, pleased he'd cared enough to speak about her to his daughter. "I can't make you any guarantees, but I'd be happy to present your photos of the Aurora to my contacts."

A hint of red tinted his tan skin, but he didn't get an opportunity to reply before the guy ahead of her completed his business and allowed her to advance. Though disappointed to have to tear her attention away, she questioned the clerk, "Is the shuttle around to give me a lift to pick up my rental vehicle at the airport?"

"I'm sorry, but it was just called over there. Since our other one is under repair, you'll have to wait for it to return. It shouldn't be longer than half an hour."

Lorelei sighed, with her phone displaying nine-forty. "Okay, I'll just call ahead and make sure they hold it."

"No need for that," Mack said over her shoulder. "I have to go back that way, so I can give you a ride. Just give me a minute to check out."

Lorelei thanked him, surprised by the offer. Deep down, she wondered if she should trust a man she hadn't been acquainted with for an entire day, but she took chances throughout her career with foreigners who didn't even share her language. While chasing stories, journalists found the best assets in locals and usually had to depend on them to land the prime perspective for their reports. Besides, what kind of bad intentions could a handsome young grandfather have when he was still bursting with pride over his new grandbaby?

Not having made use of any plush commodities during his short stay, Mack's bill consisted of the nightly rate plus tax, so he took no time to settle up. Meanwhile, the cantankerous couple in the other line finally plopped a wad of cash on the counter and huffed out the door right before Mack and Lorelei exited. As she zipped her coat higher to protect her neck from the chill of the single-digit temperatures, Lorelei observed them taking their wrath out on each other. They wouldn't relent in passing the blame back and forth over who racked up the most surcharges.

"They seem like a pretty good match," Mack dryly stated.

"You're not kidding." Lorelei averted her gaze so they wouldn't target her and Mack as the next recipients of their grievances. "I didn't have a whole lot of experience with that in my family, but I've been availed to it enough in my adulthood that it discouraged me from clinging to marriage for ultimate happiness."

"It can give you that if you find the right person and go into it for the right reasons."

Embarrassed she never considered the possibility of him being married, her cheeks warmed. She reckoned the notion didn't occur to her because of the lack of a doting grandmother accompanying him or showing up in the photos. Her own grandma along with Clara and others had taught her how much grandmothers typically treasured their grandkids.

By then, they'd arrived at his silver truck, which he

unlocked and invited her to hop inside. After he loaded his luggage into the backseat of the cab and climbed behind the wheel, Lorelei braved a follow-up to his comment. "May I assume you found the right person?"

He nodded, but he manifested the same somberness he did when she broached the subject of the earthquake yesterday. "I did, and we enjoyed that happiness for nineteen years. I lost her to kidney failure in 2007. She'd battled diabetes since she was ten."

"I'm so sorry. I shouldn't have pried. Occupational hazard."

"No worries. Enough time has passed that I've accepted it. I was worried about how Halyn would deal with not having her mom around to share in our joy, but we both held up pretty well. Her wedding day hurt us most."

"I can imagine," she replied.

She pondered the various milestones when she missed her parents, like at her high school and college graduations as well as when she earned acknowledgement for her work. She always realized, however, that those occasions didn't foster quite the same sentimentality as a wedding or birth. Despite how long he waited to take the plunge into matrimony, even Harley confided his sense of loss over their absence at his and Genevieve's ceremony. As much as she adored Uncle Reed, she struggled to envision anybody but her dad escorting her down the proverbial aisle.

She shook off her downheartedness and engaged Mack in small talk over the weather and gorgeous surroundings. The Northern Lights had amused her last night, but Anchorage offered almost as many wonders under daylight. The glaciers that were silhouettes when the plane landed now stood bright on the horizon with pristine white snow glistening under the sunshine. The short drive took them by Lake Hood, where the frozen water reflected the sterling blue sky. More than a foot of snow blanketed the ground, with its diamond-like crystals enhancing everything it covered.

"All of this sunshine surprises me," she confessed. "You always hear about the constant darkness in the wintertime here."

"Up north, they have more of that, but even here, the start of the season is pretty drab. The sun rises in the late morning, and it sets by mid-afternoon. If we have clouds or fog, it feels like night all day."

Already approaching the airport, they followed the signs to the rental company where her vehicle awaited her. Like the hotel, the complex buzzed at full speed and hardly resembled the same area she arrived at ten hours ago. She recalled the pictorial history wall inside, and a part of her yearned to return to it now that she had more time and sharper concentration. Since she'd have to fight the crowd and probably go through security again, she determined to pick it up when she set off for home.

The memory evoked her conversation with the night guard and his suggestion to visit Earthquake Park. She'd intended to search for the address online but still intrigued to learn whether or not Mack had any ties to the quake, she used it as another opening to dig while she had him.

"I guess there's someplace called Earthquake Park nearby. Have you ever gone?"

"I can't say I have."

His matter-of-fact manner yet vague tone once again discouraged her from entertaining the subject further.

The underlying journalist in her nudged her, reminding her she only had a few more fleeting moments with him and nothing to lose. "I'll find it on my GPS. If you know anybody with a survivor's perspective who'd be willing to meet me for an interview, please send them my way. I'll be here until next Wednesday."

He nodded in agreement, but his demeanor offered her no hope that he'd follow through. She encountered similar reluctance numerous times along her career, but her recent exchanges with Uncle Reed and Gabe made it seem like all men entered a strange pact of silence against her.

Mack parked right across from the doors that led to the rental company's counter. When she began to hand him some cash for his trouble, he waved it away. "I was headed in this direction, anyhow. I probably didn't lose ten minutes, tops."

"Well, then, take it for the photos of the Aurora you're going to email me," Lorelei insisted with a wink.

He grinned. "I appreciate you recovering my camera yesterday so I could take them."

"That would've been an even worse tragedy to lose those precious baby pictures."

When she hopped out of his truck, she mused over how much they'd shared in eighteen hours. If any onlookers paid attention to them, they'd likely deduce she and Mack were old friends. Oddly enough, an ache stung her in the heart, as if she were saying goodbye to just that. Nonetheless, she strove to stay in the confines of their actual status of being virtual strangers while she said her farewell.

"Thank you again for your time. Have safe travels home."

"You, too," he replied.

She sensed that he reciprocated her sadness over parting, but she didn't let her thoughts linger on the notion. Just the same, she continued to peer at the truck until it faded into the surrounding traffic, contemplating what kind of relationship they might've forged under different circumstances.

****

The rental car company handed over the keys to the compact car Calvin rented for Lorelei. She didn't feel her age very often, but occasions like this reminded her that she wasn't as young and attractive as she used to be. The concierge clerk didn't offer her any exciting upgrades, like a bigger vehicle or satellite radio. Paying no mind to the unflattering reality, she ducked into the small vehicle and left the radio tuned to the classic rock station in the presets.

She set her GPS to Earthquake Park and followed the navigation through the five-minute-long journey. Turning on her signal as she approached the entrance, she assessed the curved metal beams that stood on each side of the street. She wondered the significance of them, heightening her intrigue for the adventure ahead.

Unique architecture prevailed at the tourist site, with a concrete stair-like structure greeting the park's visitors. The first of many descriptive signs was mounted on the façade, and she studied each with rapt fascination. They gave depth to all of her research and the accompanying landmarks breathed life into the accounts that couldn't be obtained from a desk thousands of miles away. One of the first placards she read explained that the chunk of earth on the ground in front of her used to be located one hundred feet away and forty feet above its current place;

the impact of the quake sent it sliding down to where it now lay.

She took snaps of each marker, mainly for future reference. As she ventured along, she kept wondering if her Uncle Reed had taken those same steps. While gazing at the old photographs displayed around the area, however, she figured that he hadn't been able to, considering the disarray back then. One plaque showed downtown Anchorage's shredded streets, similar to the images she viewed online of the devastation, and another detailed the aftermath on the Alaskan railroads.

What stood out most of all was Steep Bluff, where the land that was level before the catastrophe now sloped into a dramatic drop-off. As mind-boggling as it was to behold the quake's toll on nature, she couldn't help but think of the people's lives that were ravaged by the horrible day. It may not have killed that many, but it certainly diminished everything they knew. More than anything, it must've taken away their sense of security, especially during the weekend that followed with some fifty-five aftershocks.

During her jaunt around the park, she also marveled at the beauty that still dominated the area. Despite everything the environment had endured, the snow-covered trees and ground flourished around her, and the waters of the Knik Arm glistened in the distance. The park itself, along with its trails—one of which traveled all through Anchorage—provided exercise and enjoyment to its visitors. The place testified to the fact that any tragedy could lead to wondrous things, if given time.

Her rumination gave way to a lesson in her own world. Ever since she developed Uncle Reed's film, she grappled with guilt over his obligations to Harley and her depriving him of the life he wanted to pursue. In retrospect, they all had joyful memories as a family. Though her recent discoveries about his past caught her off guard, she couldn't doubt his love for them and what the opportunity to raise them meant to him. Sure, he probably met with moments of considering the *what ifs* and missed Nadua, but she could never believe he regretted having them altogether. She just hoped Nadua had found similar happiness with her children.

Due to the chilly temperatures, Lorelei didn't have much company...at least of the human variety. Peering around, her gaze locked onto movement in the distance. She didn't take long to register the creature before her, having just admired its stuffed relative at the airport last night. Unlike that one, this moose was very much alive and breathing, close enough that Lorelei could make out the vapors emitted from the animal's snout.

Regardless of how many times she'd witnessed a wild animal in its natural habitat, she never took the danger for granted. Prickles of fear crept along her chest, and she stepped back a few paces for good measure. Once satisfied with the distance between them, she lifted her camera to her face and zoomed in on the majestic being as he or she milled through the forest, uninhibited by the eight inches of cold snow underfoot.

With the biting breeze getting to her, she snapped the button on her collar and trekked back to the car. Right before her feet hit the pavement of the parking lot, she noticed a groundskeeper scattering ice-melt on the sidewalk. Considering he appeared to be a little older than her, she decided to approach him to learn whether he had a connection to the quake.

"Excuse me, sir. I'm doing a story to commemorate the earthquake, and I was wondering if you had a personal account you'd be willing to share?"

"I lived in Milwaukee at the time, but my wife has quite a tale to tell. She'd be happy to contribute."

Lorelei offered him her business card. "I'd love to hear it. I'm staying in the area until Wednesday, so she can let me know if we can meet up or something."

"I'm actually about to meet her for lunch if you're interested in joining us."

Lorelei accepted his invitation, but her street-smarts cautioned her not to follow him to a remote area. To her gratitude, he lived up to his benevolent demeanor, leading her to a downtown café. After they exited their vehicles, he introduced himself as Vernon Brookfield and his wife as Heidi who awaited him in a booth.

"Ms. Carmichael here is doing a story about the earthquake," Vernon explained. "I told her you had an experience she'd like to hear."

"Please, call me Lorelei."

Heidi shook her hand and allowed her to settle in before she launched into her narrative. "Well, Lorelei, I was ten years old and in third grade, living in a city down south called Cordova. Our school released us early because it was Good Friday, so my parents took my sister and me skiing on Mount Eyak. It was starting to get dark, and we needed to go somewhere for dinner. My dad and I rode the ski-lift back to the lodge, and my mom was in one behind us with my sister. Mind you, ski-lifts already terrified Mom, and we had to persuade her to get on one every time we skied."

The twinkle in Vernon's eyes told Lorelei he'd listened to the narrative countless times before. She reckoned he typically made the same interjection here. "I can't imagine my cowardly wife being the daredevil in the bunch."

Heidi elbowed her mischievous husband in jest. "My dad and I disembarked from the lift, and our feet had barely hit the ground when it started to tremble. At first, I thought I just lost my balance, and I grasped ahold of my dad to right myself. Then, everyone around us started to cry aloud in fear. Our heads swung around to see where Mom and my sister were when we realized they still hadn't landed.

"In horror, we watched as the lift shook and jostled them in the air. Initially, they continued to advance towards us, but after a moment, the operator abandoned the controls. They, along with other skiers riding it, had no choice but to hold on for dear life. Mom clutched the armrest with one hand and Ida with the other. Meanwhile, Dad was worried about landslides, so we scurried to hide under a nearby tree. I really feared it toppling over onto us, but we didn't have any safer options. Dad kept peeking over at the ski lift, but I couldn't bear to watch, with the cables overhead making snapping noises and the metal terminals creaking. I was certain Mom and Ida would be thrown from the car.

"Miraculously, we all survived. Once the quake ended, we ran to the operator station to ensure they were okay. Before long, they resumed operation of the lift long enough to get those stranded off safely, then shut it down for inspection. Suffice to say, my mother never came within twenty yards of a ski-lift again!"

"Neither did you," Vernon dryly added between sips of coffee. "I'm fortunate if I can prod you onto an escalator."

Lorelei couldn't suppress a laugh at the banter.

Undeterred, Heidi continued, "After we reunited on solid ground and tearfully embraced one another, we rushed for home because of the threat of aftershocks. Of course, everybody had the same agenda, making for a chaotic drive. Worst of all, we didn't know what damage we may encounter along the route."

"That's terrible," Lorelei expressed.

She batted away her own memories from the fire that burnt down her family restaurant and took her parents' lives. That unsettling fear bubbled back in her stomach, the same that plagued her the instant she peered across the street from their house and beheld the billowing smoke from the eatery's kitchen. The consuming apprehension stuck with her for months afterward, to the point that she didn't even want to sit around a campfire until she was in her mid-teens.

She didn't mention her ability to relate to Heidi but maintained her professionalism and focused on the story at hand. "What else do you remember from that time?"

"Well, we made it home without incident, though it was a slow go. My dad cared a lot about the neighborhood and immediately began to check on everybody he could reach. Our school was used as a shelter for areas that suffered worse impacts, and my family volunteered quite a bit. School resumed quicker than we kids anticipated, but I suppose it helped to get back to normal. We even had new classmates from the other areas, and I made a few lifelong friends from that experience."

"You should tell her about Doli Kuliktana," Vernon said.

"Oh, yes, Doli would be a great resource for you,"

Heidi said. "She and I really bonded during the rest of the schoolyear she was enrolled in Cordova, and she works for the historical society now. She and her family are natives, and they lost everything in their village. It was located down south on the ocean, and the tsunami that accompanied the quake just devastated the community. Naturally, her memories are more difficult to discuss, but she's devoted her life to make sure the victims and aftermath are remembered. I can give you her contact information."

"That would be great. What was the name of her village?"

Heidi uttered the name Lorelei hoped to hear.

"Chenega."

Chapter Seven

As she departed the diner, Lorelei snickered at her reaction to Heidi's reference to Chenega. She couldn't repress the momentary gasp she expelled, baffled at yet another connection to the remote village. She recovered well, commenting on her research and fascination over the survival stories among its residents. Springing off of that, she dropped Nadua and Makya's names and claimed a source related their account, but Heidi didn't recall them.

She planned to take a similar approach with Doli Kuliktana, driving straight over to meet her. Heidi already arranged their appointment, with Doli telling her she didn't have any pressing matters at hand. Lorelei instructed her brain not to let her heart and its curiosity dominate the interview, considering she was there for the purpose of telling Alaska's story, not just Chenega's and her uncle's.

She could only guess what Uncle Reed would do if he realized what she was pursuing at this moment. The notion made her flinch out of a bit of guilt over the fact that she was carrying on such a quest into his personal life. He had plenty of opportunity to clue her in about his trip to Alaska, but he'd withheld all mention of it. Based on the photos alone, she couldn't be convinced that he simply didn't regard it as important. Rather, she believed its high value in his heart refrained him from discussing it. Even if she didn't uncover anything about Nadua, was she invading his privacy by entertaining the questions she had?

At the same time, she remembered that up to now, she hadn't introduced the subject of Chenega. Heidi addressed it of her own accord, and Mack's reference to Evans Island came out of the blue, as well. She didn't even pry into his possible ties to Chenega. Yet, the little village seemed to be beckoning her attention, and she couldn't ignore that. While she never considered herself worthy to be part of a so-called masterplan, she couldn't overlook these tantalizing breadcrumbs the universe appeared to be scattering ahead of her.

Since the historical society didn't have an established base, Lorelei agreed to meet Doli at her home. When she arrived at the woman's suburban cottage, Doli greeted her on the threshold, her warm smile framed by rosy cheeks. Inviting her inside, Doli offered her a fresh muffin she'd just made, but Lorelei declined for now, still stuffed from lunch with Heidi and Vernon.

"Thank you for having me on such short notice," Lorelei told her after they settled into the living room.

"It's my pleasure. I appreciate anyone who shares my interest in history. I still can't get over the fact that I am history now!" She giggled. "When you lived through what I did, though, you realize right away that you are a part of history from then on. To be honest, it's surprised me how many people have already written it off as unimportant. We continue to have quakes here and there, but none of the younger generations believe a major one will happen again."

"I understand your mixed feelings. I don't think we

truly register the magnitude of past events until we age." The statement brought to mind her own search into her uncle's past. She supposed none of this would have mattered to her as much even ten years ago. She retrained her focus back to Doli's story. "How old were you when the earthquake occurred?"

"I'd just turned nine. My dad was finishing up some repairs on his fishing boat, so my brothers and I were playing on the dock when we heard the sirens going off. The commotion confused us, given that we hadn't endured such a catastrophe before. Some fishermen nearby told us to get to higher ground, so we bolted away from the pier. They were also hollering at those who hadn't docked yet, but after a certain point, they couldn't keep trying to get the message to them. They had to run, too, or else they wouldn't have survived, either. It was very sobering to witness those unsuccessful attempts. At the time, we could only wish it wouldn't be as traumatic as it seemed."

Doli swallowed hard, not needing to say that it was as horrible as they could imagine. After a moment, she regained her composure. "All too soon, the sirens were dwarfed by the loud grinding noise that accompanied the quake. All of us huddled together at the nearest house we could get to. We watched the ground roll in agitated waves, then open and close beneath the buildings. We heard the beams creak on the house we were relying on for protection, but what else were we to do? The church itself split apart, so we held out no hope for our survival."

Lorelei dabbed away a tear, hardly able to fathom the sight, especially through the eyes of a nine-year-old. "But you and your family made it?"

Doli nodded. "With little else than our lives and

each other. Since our home was at the water's edge, we lost it in the tsunami. If that wasn't devastating enough, my mom was expecting my baby sister, so my poor parents had no home for our soon-to-be family of six."

Lorelei couldn't discount the possibility of Doli's mom being acquainted with Nadua, considering they resided in the same village, both pregnant, and suffered the same tragedy. Nonetheless, she restrained her inquisitiveness until the appropriate opportunity arose.

Doli bent over to retrieve a small box next to her chair. "I figured you would want to see these few items we were able to rescue."

Under the lid lay an assortment of belongings, partly covered by debris to this day. To the family's relief, they salvaged some pages out of a photo album, which were protected by the plastic covering. Also of sentimental value, Doli's mother found a pair of baby socks she'd crocheted, and she preserved them despite the yarn being torn and unraveled in certain areas.

Continuing with the personal presentation, Doli dug out a change purse, which was in worse condition than the other keepsakes. "When we came back months later, we couldn't believe this wasn't washed away in the tsunami. My mom dropped it when we were fleeing the pier. Even though it appears shoddy, it contains a two-dollar bill and some loose change inside that almost looks new."

With her permission, Lorelei snapped shots of the money as well as the mementos. Doli's collection held one more valuable, which caught Lorelei's eye.

"This should interest you," Doli assumed correctly of the old camera. "My father was going to surprise my mom with this for the new baby, but it sustained too much damage to operate. They saved it regardless. As a matter of fact, a news photographer gifted his spare model to them once they told him about the loss."

Lorelei's ears perked up. "Do you remember his name?"

"No. I wish I did."

Unwilling to let that go, Lorelei began her approach. "You said you recovered these after you returned? When did that happen?"

"We first went to Cordova, where I met Heidi, but that summer, we traveled to a shelter in Anchorage. My parents deemed it best for Mom to be there as her pregnancy progressed. One day in July or thereabouts, we had the chance to go back to the island, primarily to get closure. Mom and the others stayed behind, but I joined Dad. To me, that day was more heartbreaking than the earthquake on its own. Everything was a blur back then, but when we set foot on the only homeland we knew and realized we couldn't recapture it, the impact shook us to our core."

The words in Uncle Reed's letter about the Chenega natives' voyage home resonated through Lorelei's mind. Could this have been the same trip he took with Nadua? The timing sounded about right, and his presence would've enabled him to hear about Doli's family being in need of a camera. She could envision him taking a spare on this important assignment, considering he would have limited means if his primary camera failed him. Might Doli recall him if Lorelei tried to trigger her memory?

To her gratitude, Doli gave her a few minutes to debate her ethical dilemma when she rose to take a phone call. As she contemplated her position, she soon reasoned that she was making this a bigger deal than it needed to be. In light of the research she'd indeed done, why not just treat Uncle Reed's writings as a source she consulted for this? She didn't even have to offer his last name or disclose their relation. She could simply present it as a story that fascinated her, and she wouldn't be lying.

Once Doli retreated to her armchair, Lorelei executed her strategy. "Your account reminds me of an article I read to prepare for this. It related a story about a woman from Chenega named Nadua Macawi. She was also pregnant and had a little boy, Makya. Were you acquainted with them?"

Doli's face lit up. "Oh, yes, our families palled around quite a bit. We didn't know one another very well before the quake, but we stuck pretty close afterward. As you can imagine, Nadua and my mother were concerned about their babies and sought treatment from the same physicians along our whole sojourn. Nadua was actually the one who suggested we go to Anchorage together. Her baby was due two weeks after Mom's, and Makya was close to my brother's age."

Lorelei caught her breath, baffled she managed to uncover such a close link to Nadua this quickly. "Did you guys keep in touch?"

"For a while." Doli's hesitant tone made Lorelei brace for her eureka moment to evaporate at the rapid rate it'd materialized. "After a year or so, she moved southward with the kids, mostly to please her brother-in-law. He was one of the Alutiiq tribe's chieftains, so he had strong feelings about staying with the tribe and establishing a new home. Of course, it took them twenty years to get settled on Evans Island. I'm not sure if they made it there, but I'd imagine they did. When they left, he was trying to coerce her to marry him, at least according to my mom when we talked about it years later. For our part, we used relief funds from the government to buy a home in Anchorage, and since Dad already found work, we settled up here."

A range of emotions coursed through Lorelei over the narrative. A part of her was satisfied the widow had somebody to help her with her young children, given Uncle Reed couldn't fill that role. At the same time, her heart ached for her uncle and his failure to find love again, when Nadua probably married not too long after his departure. She picked up the way Doli said the brother-in-law *was trying to coerce her*, however, giving her the impression it was more of an arranged union for practicality and tradition instead of love.

Lorelei brimmed with countless questions, but they could've undermined her professionalism and wasted both of their time. To maintain her original stance, she told Doli, "Her story just captivated me, being a young, expectant widow. It's tragic. You can't help but wonder what became of her family."

"I have, too. Of all the resources I've used and helped create, I haven't run across those names."

Lorelei couldn't resist testing her memory once more. "Speaking of names, do you happen to remember a reporter named Reed something? It was his article that mentioned Nadua. I just can't place his last name right now."

"Oh, yes, Reed gave us his camera. My goodness, I haven't thought about him in eons. He and Nadua spent a lot of time together, so I'm not surprised he included her in the piece. Reed was the one glimmer of light for all of us during that dark period. I would love to read his article if you wouldn't mind sending it to me."

****

Swiping her key card in the door, Lorelei moseyed into the hotel room and collapsed onto the bed. She had to marvel at how much she'd accomplished inside of her first twenty-four hours in Alaska and the aid she garnered for both her article and her covert quest into the past. Though Doli couldn't offer her more about Nadua or Uncle Reed, she gave her several more contacts with insight into the earthquake. She directed her to a colleague in the Earthquake Alliance and a local university's archives, both of which were on Calvin's recommendation list, even lining up appointments tomorrow. She always worried she wouldn't have enough time on assignments with a fixed schedule, but that didn't appear to be a threat on this one.

She glanced over at the folder of Uncle Reed's letters on the desk and grinned about Doli's request for his article. She reckoned she'd set herself up by referencing such to a history buff like Doli, especially considering her personal connection. Lorelei hesitated for a beat until she just told her she'd have to try to locate the link in her browser history.

In light of the discoveries she made that day, she would've loved to have dug in to some more of his writings. The grimy sensation from her travels overpowered her sentimentality, however, prompting her to make a beeline into the shower. Having delayed it all day, she lingered a bit longer than usual, both to wash away the germs from the people-infested places she'd been as well as to relax her tight muscles. Though she still loved flying to distant locales, the long flights left her muscles more stoved-up nowadays.

After she emerged from the bathroom, her phone notified her of a missed call from Uncle Reed. It alarmed her somewhat, considering it was going on ten o'clock in Sedona, later than he'd stayed awake since becoming an octogenarian. She worried he might be in some sort of crisis, possibly unable to remember she was away.

"Is something wrong, Uncle Reed?" she greeted him the instant he answered her return call.

"I was about to ask you the same question," he replied, his smile obvious in his tone. "I've waited all day for your traditional call to let me know you landed safely."

Truth be told, she'd stopped apprising him of her travel updates long ago, unless she was headed to visit him. She couldn't determine if he'd forgotten that or just didn't realize she had. Despite their regular contact, she didn't let on how often she was on the go, so she neglected to alert him every time she touched down somewhere. Nonetheless, she played along. "I'm sorry. My flight landed so late last night, and I had to hurry out this morning in order to secure the rental car. After that, I've barely had a moment to myself. This is one of those stories where the leads are finding me."

"I see. You're too successful to remember your old uncle," he teased her.

If only he knew. She had to suppress the laughter over the irony of it. "How could I ever do that? He taught me everything I know about sniffing out the truth."

"And he's forgotten most of it! Speaking of which, I don't recall where you said you were going."

He was still better at nosing around for the truth than he realized. The very inquiry had refrained her from touching base with him earlier. She hated to lie to him, but she feared mentioning Alaska would trigger another episode. She couldn't bear to inflict such on him, much less with her so far away. "I'm up in Canada. My story is about natural disasters, and they've had their share in recent years, with the wildfires and whatnot."

"It doesn't seem like you'd have to travel that distance for a topic like that," he remarked. "When California's not burning, it's quaking."

His sharpness slayed her, making her grin. Just the same, her nerves tensed much like they used to when she endeavored to cover up teenage escapades in high school. "My editor has specific events he wants me to highlight. I interviewed a couple of survivors, and accounts like theirs never cease to rivet me. They talk about tragedies that happened decades ago like they occurred last week."

"We can relate, can't we? I feel like I took that phone call about your folks yesterday."

Her breath caught, shaken by the opening he gave her. He didn't address the subject but on rare occasions. Back when the first anniversary approached, he'd consulted with Harley and her about whether to mark it or treat it like any other day. They all agreed to try not to dwell on the somber occasion. From then on, they kept their conversations regarding her mom and dad confined to anecdotes about their lives, not their demises.

Considering the circumstances, she yearned to capitalize on the unusual comment and dig into his side of the story. She wanted to share her meeting with Doli and inform him of her smidgeon of insight about what Nadua did after he departed. Because of the risk to his mental wellbeing—and the threat that he'd rebuke her for her attempts to pry into his personal life—she restrained her tongue.

Instead, she fibbed again to satisfy her curiosity over the matter closest to her heart. "Don't tell Harley and Genevieve I let you know this, but they asked me if I'd take on the kids if something happened to them. I almost declined right away, given I'm not married and enjoy my freedom, but it struck me that you were in the same boat with us. You were even younger with a lot more goals and dreams ahead of you. Did you have reservations or regrets, all said and done? I'm a big girl now, so you can tell me."

A pregnant pause ensued, elapsing long enough to make her worry he was suffering another spell. Right before she panicked and asked if he was still there, he spoke up. "Lorelei Rose Carmichael, I've told you many things and hoped you'd believe most of them, but none of them rival what I'm about to say. I'd like to add that I'm of a completely sound mind at the moment, and I wouldn't dream of sparing your feelings with an untruth. Do you hear me?"

Her lips curled upward again but quivered at the same time, as she could predict where he was leading. Meanwhile, her conscience stung her for her own dishonesty. "Yes, I do, sir."

"I did hesitate when your grandmother called to ask if I'd honor the promise I made to your parents, for the reasons you just said. They made that request after Harley was born, when we were in our twenties. I meant it when I agreed, but I didn't expect to ever be in the position to fulfill it.

"Once I found myself there, the prospect scared me. I hadn't warmed up to the idea of raising a family for very long. But I combatted those insecurities, and at some point every day, I was so thankful I did. I'd look into your eyes and hear your laughter—even your brother's—and it all compensated for the sacrifices my choice entailed. It breaks my heart that we all landed in that situation, but I wouldn't trade a second of it unless I could've somehow given your parents back to you."

Her throat swelled with emotion over the touching sentiment. "Thank you for telling me that."

"I'm making up the truth this time." He chuckled. "Even so, I'm not saying you should agree to take over Harley's zoo! You'd have double what I did, and they'll probably have sticky fingers like their father."

Lorelei rolled her eyes, wondering how many cups of coffee her brother made that day with Uncle Reed's machine. She didn't dare tell him about the call she received that very morning. Given she already heard the kids were bequeathed to Genevieve's sister, she sought to conceal her fib by instructing him, "Please don't give Harley a heads-up that I looped you in on this. He's so private about his business."

After he pledged his silence, Lorelei shifted the subject to how he spent his day. His accounts about playing cards and other activities with his fellow residents encouraged her, with him recently taking up the pastimes more often than he did when he'd first moved there. She hoped he was taking to heart the counsel they received from his neurologist, that being involved in games and socializing could slow the progression of his condition. As much as she regretted leaving him at the time, she figured her absence may have motivated him to seek out other company.

She perceived his energy diminishing, but in an

effort to keep his pride intact, she expressed her own fatigue, which wasn't a lie. They wound up their conversation, as she reiterated her appreciation and love for him. Once she ended the call, her gaze returned to the stack of letters, and she couldn't resist the impulse to snatch at least one before she retreated to bed.

Gabe,

I'm enclosing my latest draft. I need you to tell me if my style is depreciating. Usually, my work improves the longer I consider a topic, but I'm afraid my vision is being clouded by personal concerns.

After we settled back into Anchorage, my relationship with Nadua deepened, and she began to reciprocate my budding devotion to her. She told me I make her feel safe amidst all of the uncertainty that plagues her. I admitted that I was falling in love with her and wanted to be there for her and Makya as more than a supportive reporter. Their story has become mine, and I don't want it to end. Regardless of how my article is received, I've already won my prize by finding them.

Little by little, we've displayed our growing affection, but those around us haven't shared our joy. The others in her tribe deem me a threat to their culture, despite my attempts to show my utmost respect for it. They believe her children would lose their connection to their Alutiiq heritage if they had a white man raising them. Worse still, Nadua's brother-in-law has made her decision for her that she should marry him to preserve the integrity of the family and tribe.

Sorry to get so personal with you lately, boss. Maybe I ought to start addressing these to Clara. I'm sure she's opening them before you, anyhow!

Although he drew a smiley face after the last

sentence, Uncle Reed's heartache remained palpable five decades after he penned the words. The despondency that pierced her when Doli discussed Nadua's possible remarriage resurged inside her, even to a more intense degree. She considered it sad enough that Nadua's brother-in-law would've pressured her to wed him after Uncle Reed departed, but the fact that he was still present made it worse yet. She longed to protect and defend her uncle from the mistreatment he encountered, but she couldn't reach that far into the past. If any of the naysayers were still around, she doubted they'd recall the damage they inflicted.

She reckoned there was a valid point in the tribe members' concerns. A colleague of hers was adopted from Peru as a toddler, and while she adored her American family, she confessed to Lorelei that she wished she had a stronger connection to her culture. Even if the controversy made sense, it must've hurt, not only Uncle Reed, but Nadua. Her world had already been upended, and the person who gave her the solace she needed faced rejection from her own people. More than that, she bore the pressure of an arranged marriage, and based on both Doli's and Uncle Reed's accounts, Lorelei inferred Nadua didn't embrace the prospect.

She empathized with Makya and his baby sibling, too, certain Uncle Reed would've raised them with the same love and commitment he bestowed to Harley and her. Race may not have factored into their upbringing, but he always struck the right balance between keeping their parents' memory alive yet treating them like they belonged to him. The picture of him with Nadua and Makya convinced her that he held them in similar esteem. As strong as her sorrow was for what they'd lost, she selfishly cherished that she had the opportunity to develop such a bond with him.

She skimmed the accompanying draft, which featured scribbles Gabe made and probably relayed to him in a follow-up. True to her uncle's self-assessment, it lacked the pop his others carried but retained a riveting and factual quality. In fact, she latched ahold of several keynotes she clamored to use in her article, but her ethics restrained her. She couldn't take his narrative as hers, nor could she credit him for remarks that were supposed to be lost in time.

Due to the note's solemnness, Lorelei didn't have a burning desire to rummage further into the envelope. Rather, she peered out of her room's window at the darkness that fell over the city hours earlier. The Aurora Borealis hadn't made its grand appearance like last night so far, but pink hues in the distance gave her hope for another meeting with the phenomena.

The thought made her wonder if Mack would oblige her entreaty for the photos he'd taken. A check of her email revealed he didn't as of yet. After clearing out the messages that didn't merit her attention, she debated which would net her the most pleasure—reacquainting herself with the Northern Lights or with Mack Holt.

Chapter Eight

Lorelei awoke Saturday morning to a pitch-black room, leaving her clueless with regards to the time. In spite of her efforts to stay up to wait for the Aurora, she fell asleep quite early the previous night. Between that and her bewildered internal clock, she wouldn't have been surprised if it was no later than three-thirty.

To her relief, her phone read *six-nineteen*, which she considered beyond acceptable for her circadian rhythm. Tossing off the covers, she rose and opened the curtains, being greeted by a dense fog that further cloaked the skyline. She hoped it would lift once the sun peeked out in a couple of hours, given she had unfamiliar routes to take for her interviews.

She followed her morning rituals, sans shower, and entered the breakfast room minutes before seven. In light of her swift start to the day, she indulged in her craving of a Belgian waffle, a childhood favorite, even if Uncle Reed had to convince her that a dab of batter could become anything edible. After she spread it inside the iron, closed the lid, and activated the switch, she checked her messages while she waited for the timer to indicate when she should flip the plate over. Mack's name graced the sender field of the top two emails, threatening to make her burn her breakfast.

Determined not to let that happen, Lorelei stuffed the phone back into the pocket of her jeans and resumed her role in the baking process. She rotated the iron at the specified intervals and ended up with the perfect amount of crispiness on each side. Once she grabbed packets of syrup and butter, utensils, and a carton of milk, she trotted to an open table, only taking one bite before she accessed her inbox again.

Mack's most recent message proved to be an apology for accidentally attaching a photo of his grandson he'd sent his sister before he composed the one to Lorelei. Deleting the unnecessary explanation, she advanced to the original email, which didn't contain much in the way of words but spoke volumes with the shots of the Aurora. He included more than she remembered him showing her at the airport, and she suspected he edited a few. Accustomed to touching up her own work, she admired those skills, as well, with it clear he made the enhancements manually instead of going with automatic filters that many amateurs employed.

She swiped through each and studied them one-by-one, appraising both their measure of talent along with the magnificence of the sight itself. Finally, she reached the one he shared by mistake, another he hadn't displayed to her the other night. No doubt snapped by his daughter, it featured baby Ahanu sleeping in the loving arms of his grandfather, who also held a small stuffed animal he might've given to the infant. Lorelei didn't examine the toy too closely, but its faded colors hinted to it being older, and its overall design gave the impression of it being homemade. She wondered if it'd been a family heirloom Mack passed down to the next generation.

Before long, guilt prompted her to close the image,

in view of the fact that he didn't intend for her to receive it. For that reason, she chose not to address it in her reply, even though she itched to commend the tender pose and inquire about the toy's origin. She concentrated on those of the Northern Lights, offering some well-deserved compliments and doubling down on her invitation to recommend him for professional projects. She wanted to say more than the three sentences she typed, but his brevity stymied her.

Lorelei perused his message a little longer after she sent hers, scouting out any more clues into his background. The signature on the bottom provided his phone number and email address, making her realize he never mentioned where he presently lived. Other than stating that he grew up on Evans Island, he didn't indicate anything about his home, not even disclosing how long of a drive he had in store yesterday. Considering he stayed at the hotel for a night, she reckoned he didn't reside very close to Anchorage, but she didn't recall him slipping a general direction into their exchanges.

She drummed it into her head that it didn't matter, that they probably wouldn't cross paths ever again, regardless. Even so, she couldn't stop her hands from fishing his contact card out of her wallet in order to discern whether or not it revealed any other identifiers. To her disappointment, it listed the same information his signature did. As a last resort, she keyed his number into a reverse phone number search, but it only reported that it was a mobile phone and notated the carrier he used.

She didn't bother to investigate the area code it had, with the explosion of communication methods making that equally as difficult to narrow down. Resigned that they wouldn't have further interaction unless he wanted more work, she retrained her focus back to her scrumptious meal. Upon lowering her gaze to her plate, she regretted her disengagement from the pleasure, as she'd already polished off almost three-quarters without savoring it like usual. It reminded her why she tried not to scroll and eat, with her wanting to enjoy every nibble if she gave in to her sweet tooth.

After taking her last bite, Lorelei disposed of her trash and moseyed back to her room to collect what she needed for the day. Along her way, she reflected on her gleanings from the day before about her uncle. Even if her quest didn't lead her to the whole truth about him and Nadua, she embraced the insight she'd gained into the man who raised her.

Considering the treatment he encountered from the tribe, she now understood his firmness regarding the way they interacted with people of all races and backgrounds. Being among Native Americans along with other cultures, he taught them to be attuned to others' sensitivities and to take the initiative to make them feel welcome. If he sensed even the smallest twinkle of a prejudiced opinion in them, he didn't hesitate to counsel them over it. That unbiased mentality influenced her approach during her many experiences with people of different nationalities.

In sorting through her memories, she endeavored to pinpoint any indicators of his history with indigenous people. Since he practiced what he preached, he always manifested the same qualities with them as he did anybody else. She couldn't remember an occasion when he exhibited favoritism toward or against them. He employed different ones for various services, but he never behaved in a way that let on to this relationship he had with Nadua…unless Lorelei was too ignorant to perceive it.

As she unlocked the door to her room, the click of the handle's latch matched the one in her brain. All of a sudden, she envisioned her first and most beloved family pet—an Alaskan Husky named Hope. Uncle Reed surprised the kids with it when they were teens, and although he claimed she was a gift meant to teach his niece and nephew responsibility, he adored her. He took Hope everywhere with him, including to the office if he had a brief task to perform. She lived past Lorelei's college graduation, and both she and Harley worried Uncle Reed would need antidepressants to cope with the grief of having to put her down.

Given everything she'd uncovered in recent weeks, Lorelei couldn't dismiss the breed as a coincidence. She hadn't found reason to believe Nadua owned a Husky or anything, but she had to wonder if the nod to the state and culture furnished him with a subtle attachment to her. On the few instances he entertained adopting another dog, he only considered that breed. In the end, however, he didn't take one on, much like he never pursued a serious relationship after his romance with Nadua.

Retrieving her bag and camera to take with her to her interviews, she did her best to tuck away all of the speculation about Uncle Reed and to recalibrate her focus onto work. The texts awaiting her from Cal helped with that, as he wanted to learn if she'd touched base with any of the contacts he gave her. His hovering irritated her a bit, considering she relished the freedom in her position as a *free*lance journalist. Nonetheless, she figured he had the right to be more involved, taking into account what he agreed to pay her.

She took a few minutes to assure him that she had two of his recommendations on her schedule for the day. By the time she finished, she needed to set out for the first one with the representative of the Alaska Earthquake Alliance. Not brightening her spirits, the fog still hung low and almost seemed thicker than earlier. Still, she forged ahead, albeit at a slower pace to compensate for the lack of visibility.

For any interview—including controversial ones— she didn't take for granted the interviewee's willingness to participate. While most of her pieces revolved around her photos, she needed insight and context to add the authenticity she strove to reflect. In a world where people took a "no comment" stance about everything outside of social media, she valued those who gave her a few moments, especially on a weekend.

Doli arranged for Lorelei to meet Stan Meadows at the fire station. The woman explained he was a third-generation firefighter and was very active in the Earthquake Alliance because of his father's life-saving actions in the 1964 quake. She didn't elaborate any further into his story, though, designating that honor to him.

She met up with him in the chief's office. From the crow's feet around his eyes, she deemed him to be around her age, but his physical profession carved his muscles into those of a younger man. With a nice head of dark hair, she assumed he must've appeared in a calendar or two if the Anchorage department made them. She stopped her gaze from lingering any longer after she spotted his wedding ring.

Their conversation proved enriching to more than the eyes, with Stan offering both the resources from the Alliance along with his own observations. On his tablet, he showed her some rare video footage of the quake captured by a local filmmaker and a few clips of news coverage. To her gratitude, he also gave her copies of several news clippings from the time period.

Aside from that, Stan presented her with a catalog of photos she had never run across on the Internet. Chronicled by region, it included many from Anchorage and Seward, and her heart leapt when a label read *Chenega*. The section only contained four images, with three showing the damage to the landscape similar to some she saw before. The one that interested her most, however, featured a group of men appearing to be convened in some sort of meeting. All white men, she didn't reckon Nadua or her tribe would've been involved, but she still wondered if their conference impacted Nadua in any way.

Hoping her winning streak would continue, she tapped on the section and questioned Stan, "Did your father have any experiences on this island? I've read a lot about the toll they suffered there."

Stan shook his head. "Dad didn't get assignments out that far, but a few in his squad did. They had some pretty harrowing war stories."

Why couldn't she have had the opportunity to interview their children? Remembering that her story needed to include more than her research into Chenega, she set her mind back onto her true objective. "Tell me more about your dad's experiences in his rescue efforts."

"Dad piloted the department's helicopter, so for the first couple of weeks, he was in charge of getting into the remote areas to try to locate missing people. He could never get over how far some had navigated from where they were assumed to be. People just had to run for their lives, and the adrenaline often kept them from realizing how far they made it. Besides that, he and his team recovered several who had fallen into chasms where the earth opened up and basically swallowed them. Thankfully, the majority didn't get too buried and managed to survive it."

"How old were you at the time?"

"Four, so as you'd imagine, a lot of my memories are more from the accounts I was told later rather than from the actual event. I remember the shaking of my bedroom and relocating to my grandparents' house for a month, but the rest is blank."

"Growing up among other victims, did it stick with you and your peers, always in the recesses of your thoughts?"

Seeming to sort through his past, he took a moment to contemplate his reply. "Speaking in generalities, I suppose we had a heightened awareness of how fragile life is and that you couldn't take even standing on solid ground for granted. Some have had to cope with lifelong anxiety disorders, especially those who lost loved ones. For the most part, though, we just shared a mutual understanding of what happened, and we didn't delve very deeply into each other's tales. Even when somebody only had one living parent, we held back from inquiring whether or not the quake was the reason."

Lorelei wished she could've had that kind of silent agreement with her classmates, instead of being badgered with curiosities about why her uncle was her guardian. "Is that unspoken pact still intact even now?"

He made a gesture between a nod and a shrug. "Our conversations don't revolve around it by any means, but a lot of us have opened up a bit more. I think a part of it has to do with the older generation passing away. After I lost my dad, I joined the Alliance, mostly because his death opened up a void in me. I missed that connection to him and everything he did for the community. Plus, the younger ones lack the insight into what happened and don't maintain the needed diligence to prepare for it occurring again."

Lorelei appreciated the passion he displayed and could've written a piece on him alone if the assignment had called for it. Regretting that she wouldn't be able to exploit his knowledge to the degree she would've liked to, she grasped for the best manner in which to showcase him. Without her clueing him in on her quandary, he provided her with the solution when he revealed that he carried his father's badge with him. Being a pilot as well, he even wore the same headset every time he flew. To her delight, he agreed to let her photograph him with both.

After she finished up, she headed to the university to take a look at their collection of artifacts. During her drive, she pondered everything Stan related to her about the reactions and long-term effects the earthquake had on young survivors. This whole experience had changed her mentality in so many ways. When she reported on various disasters through her career, she cared about those affected, but she couldn't claim she continued to consider how they were coping in the following months and years. Sadly, the frequency of natural and man-made disasters desensitized her as much as the majority of bystanders. Though her line of work gave her an ideal vantage point of such events, it also demanded that she forge ahead rather quickly, moving on to the next project. She supposed her age altered her perspective, but she attributed most of the transformation to her discovery of Nadua's story.

Being a Saturday, the university's parking lot had plenty of open spaces, so Lorelei took one close to the history building. She already made contact with Winnie Denton, the head of the archives department who Doli recommended. Winnie instructed her to give her a call when she arrived so that she could get her into the building and escort her to the correct room.

A native woman, Winnie greeted Lorelei with a bright smile and welcomed her to the campus. As they navigated through the hallways, Lorelei admired the nods to the local culture in the decorum. Indigenous tapestry hung on the walls, along with carvings of an array of scenes related to the heritage. She wanted to take snapshots of them, if not for the article but for her own safekeeping. She didn't take the chance, as Winnie chatted with her the entire way, asking her a number of questions about her work and article.

Winnie led her into a spacious library, where she approached a bookcase in one corner. Lorelei anticipated a row or two to be devoted to the earthquake, so her mouth hung agape to discover that scores of shelves housed contents about the event.

"I'm only here until Wednesday!" she joked to Winnie.

"We're challenging the Internet to acquire the wide collection we boast," she replied. "We've had the privilege of collaborating with other museums and such. Local survivors have donated their stash of pictures, personal correspondence, newspaper clippings, and even some audio and video material. We also have legal documents and governmental notices if you're interested. If you can tell me what would best fit your piece, I can point you in the right direction."

Despite the goldmine before her, despondency befell Lorelei, since she'd already amassed a lot of the items Winnie mentioned. While she needed some historical background with which to season her article, the majority had to spotlight present-day conditions. In truth, she'd worried about wasting hers and others' time, but she didn't want to dismiss Doli's kindness. Besides, Cal suggested she utilize the university, as well.

Without any other to-dos on her itinerary for now, she opted to hunker down and hope something sparked inspiration. "It's overwhelming. Why don't I peruse a little by myself and then consult you from there? I'd just like to get my bearings."

"I completely understand. I need to return a call anyhow, so I'll do that and stand by if you need me."

Lorelei thanked her and wandered alongside the bookshelves, skimming the titles of published biographies and binders that contained the more personal artifacts. She selected one of the binders that featured a married couple's collection and began to leaf through it, but her ears betrayed her by tuning into Winnie's phone conversation. She'd never been one to eavesdrop, so she couldn't comprehend why this stranger's exchange ignited her inquisitiveness.

"Is everything okay with Mom?" Winnie questioned almost right away. Her intonation made Lorelei ascertain the other person may have been a sibling. "Yeah, she missed you. How was your trip?"

Lorelei pried her attention away from the business that didn't concern her. She was surprised by how close it mirrored her circumstances, between the reference to a sick or aging parent and the comment about a trip. With it similar to her call to Harley the previous day, she would've burst into giggles—and maybe goosebumps—if the discussion shifted to a coffee maker.

Even though it didn't take that twist, she couldn't believe her ears when they registered Winnie saying, "The photos you sent of the baby were adorable. Halyn looks so happy…and tired, of course."

Halyn? Wasn't that the name of Mack's daughter?

After a pause, Winnie continued, "I see a lot of her and Ewa in him. I'm sure 'Ahanu' will suit him eventually."

She might be able to pass off the two unusual names strung together as coincidence, but considering she had just uttered a similar statement about another baby, she could only draw one conclusion: Winnie was talking to Mack.

****

Lorelei tried to shake off her theory about Winnie and Mack being related, training her gaze onto the bookshelves. Her brain commanded her tongue not to ask or say anything to Winnie after she hung up in an attempt to investigate further, aware she would sound nosey and perhaps bonkers. Whether or not Mack was the other person on the line shouldn't matter to her.

The conversation didn't last very long, with Winnie neglecting to state the recipient's name before they ended the call. Like a child who didn't want to be caught goofing off in class, Lorelei did her best to appear immersed in her studies. Just the same, Winnie drifted back toward her.

"Once you're at a stopping point, we have an exhibit near the circulation desk I'm confident you'll enjoy."

Lorelei didn't hesitate to take her up on it, trailing her over to a wall of paintings.

"These are on display for the commemoration of the fiftieth anniversary. The artist is a staff member here, and he used some debris from a dump that was used back then in his materials."

Lorelei examined the works of art, which portrayed bleak scenes of people navigating the destruction and the losses they suffered. She wouldn't decorate her home with the sober images, but she had to marvel at the intricate craftsmanship along with the profound way the artist captured the survivors' agony. "This is incredible."

"He took a crude approach on purpose to illustrate the hardship on those impacted and how their lives were so rudimentary as they had to start over," Winnie explained.

"Each piece definitely demonstrates that," Lorelei replied. "I'd love to talk to him if he's available."

Winnie scrunched her face. "You said you're leaving Wednesday? Unfortunately, he's away for a conference this whole upcoming week. I can pass along your information to him, though, if you'd like to do a phone interview or something."

"That would be great. My deadline isn't for a few weeks, so I'll have time to include his thoughts. If you don't mind, I'll snap some shots and ask him for permission to use them."

"Go ahead. We have no rights to them."

Lorelei unpacked her equipment and proceeded with her work, taking a few close-ups as well as some wide-angle shots of the corridor. She asked Winnie, "Would you like to pose for one? Your role here has done a lot to keep the earthquake's memory alive."

"I'd be honored if you would like that," Winnie said.

Lorelei staged one of her with the exhibit and another by the bookcase that housed all of the references to the subject. The whole while she aimed the camera, she kept discerning the characteristics that seemed similar to Mack. She couldn't determine if she was making it up because of her notion of them being related, but she recognized a resemblance around her forehead and nose. The smile, though, was the most convincing proof, as Lorelei couldn't forget the captivating quality that Mack and his daughter shared, too.

Her heart yearned to seek confirmation of her speculation, and she remained hopeful Winnie might allude to her brother having an interest in photography. To Lorelei's disappointment, she said nothing in that vein. In view of how little she brought up any of Harley's hobbies, she didn't deem it unusual. Still, she couldn't shed her relentless wonderings.

"Did you have personal experience with the quake?"

Winnie's smile faded a notch. "I wasn't around yet when it struck, but I've witnessed the aftermath. Some of my relatives perished, and our homeland was all but destroyed."

"What area?"

"Chenega," Winnie stated, which made Lorelei want to smile with delight, but she restrained her lips so as not to appear insensitive. "It was a coastal village close to the epicenter. What really hurt us was the accompanying tsunami. It wiped out a third of our residents."

"I've read about that," Lorelei replied. "How awful. I'm so sorry for you and your family."

"Thank you."

"Just reading the accounts breaks your heart enough, but to live it is unimaginable."

Sadness cloaked Winnie's face, making Lorelei cringe over the way she pressed her. She reflected on Stan's words about people's silence about their losses and regretted having to undermine that. Then again, Winnie's position required her to discuss it often, so maybe it didn't bother her.

"Did your losses inspire you to get into this kind of career?" Lorelei asked.

"To a degree. Teaching was my dream, and I've always loved history. When the university hired me, another professor ran the archives, but the dean offered me the job after he retired because of my background. Some may consider it odd that I'd take it on since it was a tragedy that cost us so much, but I view it as an opportunity to honor them."

"Could I quote you on that?" Lorelei implored her.

Winnie gave her permission, adding "I'm happy to assist you however I can. Do you have a specific topic you'd like to explore more in-depth?"

Lorelei refrained from giving her internal response, which was Uncle Reed and Nadua's love story, and kept on her journalist hat. "My editor would like a good mix of comparison photos of the changed landscape along with some of survivors, maybe then and now. I visited Earthquake Park yesterday and took a nice variety of the shifts in the land. I'm hoping to incorporate as many of the affected areas as I can."

Winnie nodded, contemplative. "If you'd like, I

could try to get ahold of some who I've worked with over the years and ask if they're agreeable to participating."

Exhilaration surged through Lorelei. "I'm grateful for any help I can get with the legwork. Thanks very much."

"You're welcome. I doubt I could get you all the way to Chenega, but I can see if I can coerce any of my family or friends to be involved. If you're available tomorrow, I'd be happy to give you a tour of several sites that aren't too much of a distance."

Lorelei's mind struggled to keep up with the swiftness of all this, with it seeming like a dream. "That would be fantastic. I'm more than willing to compensate you for your time."

Winnie waved a dismissive hand. "My kids are on a trip with their dad, so you're sparing me a lonely weekend at home."

The ladies hashed out their arrangements, after which Winnie played one of the audio recordings of news broadcasts she referred her to earlier. With her unable to include any of it, Lorelei listened mostly to satisfy her own curiosity. That said, the downhearted yet urgent tones of the reporters gave her a realistic feel of the frantic state of affairs, amplifying the vivid narrative she hoped to convey.

Though Winnie couldn't join her, she recommended a bakery to Lorelei, where a clock hung that had been ticking during the quake and somehow continued to work up till now. Along with that, she assured her that the goodies prepared there didn't disappoint. Having already indulged in the waffle for breakfast, Lorelei gave her sweet tooth a pep talk on the drive there, hoping it would remain satisfied by the earlier splurge.

Once engulfed in the wafts of fresh pastries, real European chocolate, and cookies, however, her irresistible cravings silenced all of her intentions to show self-restraint. She chose to believe her late grandmother's doctrine that vacation calories didn't count. Besides, she reasoned the bakery wouldn't appreciate her stopping by just to photograph a clock without purchasing anything.

With it being lunchtime, she steered her yearnings in a healthier direction, opting to get a taste of the aromatic pastries through one of the restaurant's meat wraps. The menu presented typical meat choices, but it also displayed an uncommon option—reindeer. Early on in her career, she maintained a more selective palate, afraid of getting sick in remote locales. Uncle Reed would always ask her what kind of foreign dishes she'd eaten on assignments and lightheartedly rib her about sticking to American staples. His teasing eventually coaxed her to be more adventurous, so nowadays, the unfamiliar entrees ended up being her top pick.

True to her acquired style, she ordered the reindeer sausage with cream cheese Dijon wrap. One patron stood behind her, so she didn't ask the cashier about the clock as she passed through the line. While she waited for her lunch, she took a gander around the eatery and spotted an antique timepiece on the wall near the kitchen. The woman who followed her only bought a rhubarb strudel—which she coveted the instant she observed the cashier wrap and serve it. After she exited with her treat, Lorelei approached the worker to learn what she knew.

She pointed at the clock. "I heard one of your clocks survived the 1964 earthquake. Would that happen to be the one?"

The woman beamed with pride. "Yes, it sure is, but I'm not the one to talk about it. Let me get my mom for you."

She disappeared into the kitchen and returned with an older woman moments later. "I'm Inga. I hear you're fascinated with my clock."

"Yes, it's beautiful. I'm more interested in the story behind it, though."

She wore the same grin as her daughter. "That is quite a doozy, I must say. If you're dining here, why don't we share a table and discuss it over your lunch?"

Happy to oblige, Lorelei allowed her to pick their spot while she waited for her meal. Once the cook presented it to her, she studied the unusual sandwich on the plate and wondered if it would be a mistake having the owner across from her as she tried it. Despite branching out with her culinary choices, she still feared how her system would react to the foreign varieties and never wanted to manifest her dislike of anything. She was especially sensitive around those who prepared the dish. For good measure, she decided not to admit that this was her first taste of reindeer so that her host wouldn't scrutinize her response to it.

She carried the tray to the table Inga had claimed, which overlooked the clock. As she sat down, she realized that the off-kilter circumstances of their meeting caused her to forget her manners. "I'm Lorelei Carmichael, by the way, and I'm writing an article about the fiftieth anniversary of the earthquake."

"I can't wrap my head around it being that long ago. My husband and I hadn't lived here for very long before it struck; we moved from Switzerland earlier that year. Talk about a welcoming! Because of the climate back

Karina Bartow

home, we didn't have any qualms about the weather, but we never expected an event like that. It shook us, literally and metaphorically."

Lorelei smiled and returned Inga's wink, delighted by her witty personality. "Had you already opened the bakery?"

"Oh, no. My husband, Gerald, worked in other shops, honing his skills for ages before he bought this place. This was a retirement job of sorts. I wish he would've lived longer to witness how much it's flourished, but it fulfilled him during the time he was here. He wanted a legacy to pass down to our daughter and her children, and he did enough legwork to secure that much."

Her candidness prompted Lorelei to open up. "That's very special. My parents had a restaurant in Boston and hoped for the same for my brother and me, but it burned down when we were small."

"I hope nobody was hurt." Though warm, Inga's sentiment came across as a statement rather than a question, so Lorelei didn't bother to tell her otherwise. "Don't let me keep you from eating."

Not wanting to be rude, Lorelei swallowed her reservations as she picked up the sandwich. She bit into it, steeling her face in an attempt not to indicate any negative thoughts. She analyzed the flavor while she chewed, with it reminding her a bit of the venison Harley made for her after a hunting trip years ago. She wouldn't term it very gamey, especially with the sausage's spices dominating the flavor like most summer sausages. The cream cheese Dijon gave it an unexpected but tasty tang.

Relieved she could offer a genuine compliment, she confessed to Inga, "I've never had reindeer before. This is a delicious introduction."

"I'm glad we had the privilege of acquainting you two. Like all of our other dishes, it's very popular in Europe, namely Norway. For years, the locals would correct us that it should be caribou, but there's a difference. Just because we're here doesn't mean we have to change our recipes," Inga said. "Back to the clock, some relatives of mine gave it to us for our wedding, so it was a fixture in every home we had. Gerald hung it in the living room of our rental house just a week or two before the earthquake, and I heard it fall in all of the commotion that evening. We ended up evacuating because of the damage and threat of aftershocks, and neither of us even thought to collect it or clean up the mess it must've created.

"When we returned, I was sweeping up the broken glass and whatnot from the frames and lamps that had shattered on the floor. I grabbed hold of it with one hand and had the broom in my other, but as I readied to resume my sweeping, I discovered there wasn't any shrapnel left behind." She began gesturing to mimic the experience. "I whipped my head around and beheld that the face of it didn't have a crack on it. A couple of scratches tarnished it, but that was nothing to us."

"How amazing," Lorelei replied.

"I examined it for days, trying to find the hairline crack that promised to spider-web, but it never manifested." She shook her head at the memory. "At that point, we'd been debating retreating back to Switzerland because of the terror of everything and already having to start anew yet again. Once we discovered that clock, though, its resilience emboldened us that we could forge onward. We could remain intact as a unit and keep ticking together, as we liked to put it.

"It became a symbol of our love and commitment to stabilize each other no matter what earth-shaking catastrophes befell us. We took it everywhere with us, until we hung it right up there. Opening this place, too, was a risk, and few believed it would pay off because 'no one would pay for real butter and chocolate' like Gerald wanted to serve. I told him that whenever he caught a glimpse of it as he worked, he needed to remember that those naysayers didn't rival what we'd weathered in the slightest."

Lorelei gazed at the clock with a newfound appreciation. "That's lovely. We all need a symbol of hope like that."

"I agree. If you ask me, everyone can find one if you look hard enough, regardless of what you might endure. All of us have a keepsake of some kind that we preserve often without giving it much thought, but when we reflect on what it's seen along with us through the years, we have to marvel at it. So much comes and goes— whether by design or not—but that has stuck by us, even if it's stowed away."

Lorelei smiled. *Like a roll of undeveloped film.*

Chapter Nine

Lorelei sat on the hotel bed and admired the shots she'd taken that day. She treasured the one of Inga standing by the clock and was already drafting the portion of her article that she would devote to her and her husband's story. Once again, she wished she had more room to spotlight each individual account. Like many, she threw around the idea of writing a book after she retired, and if she ever did, Inga's life seemed like good inspiration...behind Uncle Reed and Nadua's, of course.

Following her visit to the bakery, she did a little shopping nearby to grab a few supplies she forgot to pack in her suitcase before she left home. With all that she had accomplished since landing, and the promise of tomorrow's sightseeing tour with Winnie, she could expel a mental sigh for a change. Even now, she wouldn't fret over a lack of material if she had to fly back to Arizona tonight. If Winnie provided as many resources as she hinted at, Lorelei could enjoy a couple of days of leisure to cap off her trip if she wanted.

Finishing off the chocolate-dipped cookie Inga insisted she take on her way out, Lorelei tossed the wrapper into the garbage can beside the desk and gazed at the stack of Uncle Reed's letters. Still pondering the one she read last night about the tribe rejecting him, she didn't yearn to scour through them like she did earlier. Plus, her knowledge of the way it no doubt ended made her sad to watch the stack dwindle away. She couldn't help but brace herself to relive her parents' death, afraid that would be the subject of Uncle Reed's final correspondence.

Not too tired yet, she slid the top one out of its envelope and began reading. Her uncle displayed a cheerier mood than before, and she wondered if matters really improved in the ten days between letters or if he was growing self-conscience about confiding in Gabe. Regardless, she gathered he and Nadua had made the mutual resolve to stay together in spite of the controversy around them.

Gabe,

Normalcy is still a far way off, but we're starting to see some brightening developments. A hotel has managed to re-open and taken in some of the neediest survivors free of charge. With a little persuasion, they invited Nadua and Makya to be among them, considering her fragile condition. The doctor at the shelter assisted us in moving her up on the priority list by evaluating her, from which he estimated the baby's arrival to be no more than eight weeks away.

With my article close to complete, I'm giving them most of my attention, trying to lighten her load. Now that they've left the shelter, nobody makes their meals. As I work on honing my skills, Nadua's introduced me to a few local dishes. Yesterday, she made us muktuk, meat that comes from the skin, blubber and cartilage of a whale. I trusted her because of her sensitive appetite, but I ended up sick after four bites!

Words fail to describe the flavor, which changes as it seems to war with itself in your mouth. It fluctuates between being oily, nutty, chewy, and salty. No matter the phase, I'd call it inedible but tried my best not to show my abhorrence to her. She insists it's an acquired taste, but I don't reckon I have the stomach to develop it. Somehow, I may have to, given she and Makya love it, as does the little one, if Nadua's hunger for two helpings is any indication.

Once I recovered enough, she made up for it by giving me a piece of toast with thimbleberry jam, another specialty of Alaska. A kind relief worker from up north gave her a jar from his pantry, homemade by his wife. It was tarter than any other type of jam I've tasted before, but I enjoyed it. Maybe we'll grow some on our property and send some to you and the family.

I've put the finishing touches on the article. After I receive your feedback, I'll submit it to Global Expeditions.

Lorelei snickered over the irony of her uncle pursuing the very journal who'd commissioned her for this story. He always manifested pride in her pieces they published, but he never confessed to his own brushes with them. She also gained a better grasp on his prodding her to expand her palate, having done so during his stay. At the same time, she'd like to tease him about being a hypocrite, judging by his intolerance of muktuk. She couldn't remember many occasions when he took a disliking to a dish, so she could only imagine his reaction.

This go-around, the envelope included his draft, signaling Gabe didn't provide much tweaking and may have just written the little input he had. When she examined it, she understood why, with his grammar flawless and his prose gripping. She couldn't fathom an editor rejecting such a submission, unconvinced any of her articles began to measure up to it. This should've transformed his career, catapulting him from a local reporter of a quaint bi-weekly periodical to a renowned, award-winning journalist.

After the humor of the muktuk incident waned, Lorelei's remorse resurfaced. Though the thought of him facing scrutiny and criticism pained her, it alleviated part of her guilt over being what separated Nadua and him. This uncovered the effort both of them were willing to make for their love. They were planning a life together, with Uncle Reed hinting at establishing a home and growing their own food. All her life, she cherished that they'd become a family unit, but he had that somewhere else.

Nadua and Makya were his choice, not his obligation.

Lorelei reeled in her spiraling melancholy, reasoning that she shouldn't give rise to such childish jealousy. Being the adult she was, she recognized that major decisions were typically made as a result of several different factors instead of just one. Maybe Nadua and Uncle Reed discovered they weren't all that compatible once they started to spend more one-on-one time together away from the shelter. Perhaps their difference in food choices was a precursor to more important disagreements that arise in new couples. Plus, from what Doli indicated, it seemed Nadua's brother-in-law persisted in his efforts to coerce her to preserve the family line the way he wanted. That alone could drive any couple apart.

As she returned the contents of the envelope, Uncle Reed's sentiments from the other night about having no regrets echoed through her mind. Determined to trust him, she concluded that the insights she gleaned shouldn't serve to send her into a pity party for Uncle Reed or even herself. On the contrary, they proved his devout loyalty to her, Harley, and their parents, giving her ever more reason to appreciate and love him for the sacrifice he made.

****

The next morning, Lorelei slept later than she intended, having arranged to pick up Winnie by eight o'clock. Already past seven, she'd have to hustle to make it across town to the suburb where Winnie lived. A glimpse out her window showed it to be another foggy day, making her nervous once again to navigate unfamiliar territory in this gloomy haze. She suppressed her anxiety and focused on packing some extra supplies for the long day, including a spare battery pack for her camera. Using the bag where she stored the envelope of letters, she decided to return them to the front pocket, just in case she wanted to consult them for reference.

Without time to even be tempted by the waffle iron, she opted to forego the continental breakfast altogether, which would've thrown her cheapskate brother into a tailspin. When she keyed the Oceanview neighborhood into the GPS on her phone, the estimated fourteen-minute-duration relieved her. The sun having yet to rise, it felt more like a nighttime journey than a morning one, and the fog didn't help the dreariness. It grew denser as she traveled away from the downtown district, making her more skittish about all of the driving in store.

She didn't have to wait long for Winnie to emerge from her split-level home, a mug of coffee in each hand. Lorelei ducked out of the car to free up her hand so she could open the door.

"I took the chance on you being a coffee drinker," Winnie told her. "If you're not, I'll give myself an extra dose."

"You guessed correctly. Thank you. I rushed out of the hotel without stopping for anything."

"No worries. I made a pot for myself and hated for the rest to go to waste. I've been tossing around hints about my desire for a single-cup machine, but my oblivious family hasn't picked up on the message yet." She winked. "Are you sure you don't want me to drive?"

A weight dissolved from Lorelei's stressed core. "Like I said yesterday, I don't want you using your gas and all, but I'd let you drive my rental if you wouldn't mind. Trekking through fog on roads I don't know rattles my nerves."

"I can relate. I hear they had a fresh coating of snow in that direction, so it could get slick to boot."

When Lorelei asked if it was still advisable to go, Winnie waved her off, undaunted. Being an Alaska native, she'd no doubt had to become an adept driver to trudge through the prolonged winters. The women switched sides, with Lorelei beyond content to plop down onto the passenger's seat and sip her delicious cup of Joe.

After a short time into their journey, Lorelei thanked Winnie again for offering to drive, as the dense fog still hung above them and was compounded by slushy snow that began to fall. Winnie slowed her speed and navigated the impeded visibility with proficiency. They both sighed with relief when they arrived at the first stop, the Girdwood Ghost Forest.

"I'm not sure you have a clear vision of the kind of article I'm writing," Lorelei teased after she read the name of the site on a sign.

Winnie chuckled over her reaction and suggested they wait for a beat in hopes the snow would taper off. In the meantime, she explained the significance of the woods before them. "Believe it or not, this used to be a small community before the earthquake made it uninhabitable. The Turnagain Arm is on the other side, and its waters flooded the whole area. Not only did it wipe out the residences, but it obliterated the trees. Since the bedrock dropped nine feet, the trees did, too, which allowed the saltwater to fill those craters. That killed the roots, and they never grew back."

Between the fog and the sluggish sunrise, Lorelei couldn't make out much detail of the property from her vantage point in the car. Once she learned its history, however, she noticed that the trees were bare of leaves or pine needles. She would've assumed they were just dead for the winter, but now, she recognized the bleakness of the trunks.

When the snow abated, the two bundled up and strode into the wooded area. Winnie guided her through a trail they couldn't see underneath the snowy ground, which didn't have any footprints from recent visitors. Flickers of daylight attempted to penetrate the fog, creating a hazy glow through the deserted land. Along their meandering route, they passed the abandoned structures that used to serve as homes, some only having two or three walls standing with caved-in roofs. If she hadn't known better, she would've concluded that they were sheds for hunting or storing firewood.

The trees Winnie described accentuated the grimness of the effects on the environment. Up close, they had a stark, barren appearance, quite different from a live tree that's dormant for winter. The trunks resembled plain—albeit tall—sticks that somebody drove into the ground, with only the top half of them above-ground. Some of them leaned at odd angles, their falls frozen in time.

As Lorelei snapped shots of them, Winnie told her, "This might sound crazy, but they look even stranger without the snow. Then, you can really see that the base of the trunks extend beneath the ground."

"So, the holes have filled in around them?"

Winnie nodded. "Oh, yeah. The sediment and everything has allowed grass to grow, but it's still pretty swampy. Some of the trees are sunk deeper than the rest, which has indicated that the area has fallen victim to several quakes before the one in 1964."

Lorelei murmured an acknowledgement of the sad fact and proceeded to take the last handful of photos, including one of the frozen body of water that contributed to the devastation. With the wind picking up, they hastened their retreat to the parking lot. Once inside the rental car, Winnie started the ignition as soon as she settled behind the wheel, and Lorelei cranked up the heater. Giving the engine a bit to warm up, they both savored their coffee, which still retained some heat.

Because the beverage was flavored with hazelnut creamer, she couldn't resist recounting the saga of Harley and their uncle's maker. The anecdote led to more banter about their families, which filled the majority of the first leg of their jaunt. Though Lorelei assumed Winnie was divorced from her remark about her kids being away with their dad, she learned the two were about to celebrate twenty years of marriage. Her husband, Lyndon, took her two daughters with him to his twenty-fifth college reunion, in hopes of tempting them to attend his alma mater after they graduated high school. The fact that the university was located all the way in Georgia seemed to be the reason for Winnie's irritated tone.

"Like I keep telling him, it would save us so much money for them to go to school up here. Because of my position with the university, we would save a fortune in tuition, not to mention the travel expenses of moving them and arranging visits," Winnie related. "Plus, I just can't imagine being that far away from my girls."

Lorelei made supportive comments as Winnie lamented about the difficulties of letting go of growing children, her daughters being seventeen and fifteen. Lorelei still had a hard time fathoming that she would be in the same predicament by now if she'd had a family. It didn't seem that long ago that she was touring colleges as a high schooler.

After she'd said her peace, Winnie switched the subject to Lorelei's background. Without a husband or kids, she spoke about her upbringing but remained vague about her parents' accident. She never enjoyed detailing the tragedy, and to her gratitude, Winnie didn't pry. Having lost her relatives in the earthquake, she probably understood the weight of such a traumatic event. Lorelei told her a little about Uncle Reed's recent diagnosis, wondering if she would open up about whatever was going on with her mom, but she didn't.

The whole while, she continued to listen closely for any references Winnie made that pointed to Mack being her brother. Not surprisingly, she focused a lot of her attention on her husband and kids, and Lorelei didn't try to divert the conversation any other way. She didn't want to seem like Mack's stalker and couldn't figure out how she would react if she did get confirmation of her assumption. With time's passing, she lost conviction in her hunch and reasoned that all of her romanticizing about Uncle Reed's past may have distorted her judgment.

After over an hour of driving, Winnie approached their second destination, a roadside monument in Whitter. Surrounded by a rose garden, a boulder sat with a plaque mounted to its face that spoke of the toll the disaster took on the port town. Though just over thirty miles from the epicenter, the area didn't fare too badly from the quake itself, but like Chenega, the tsunamis did the most damage. According to the report on the marker, the town lost the rail yards, a lumber mill, and a petrolatum tank farm, which burned for three days after being demolished by a massive wave.

Winnie stood beside Lorelei as they both read the memorial, and the professor's fingers stroked the words that touched her most. "Of all the stories I've heard, I consider this among the saddest. Several families were gathered in the lumber mill residents' quarter for a party, and all twelve people perished, including six children. Another infant in town was ripped out of her mother's arms. I can't even fathom it."

"Me neither," Lorelei agreed, reading the inscription to digest the fact that seven of the thirteen victims were children. "It's another reminder that the numbers don't do justice to the real story."

Winnie acknowledged the remark, and Lorelei snapped a few shots of the site. Despite not being able to connect her with any of the affected families, she took her to the property where the lumber mill used to stand, replaced by a hotel. Unlike the destitute Ghost Forest, the land now hosted a gorgeous four-story waterfront building. Gazing at it, she reflected on how life and time, for the most part, trudged ahead, with tragedies covered over by beauty and commemorated by a simple plaque.

Albeit sobering, the fact showed that mourning was supposed to lighten and give way to brighter horizons. Nobody wanted to remain a living ghost forest, dark and devoid of any natural beauty. She appreciated that Uncle Reed had facilitated such a process for Harley and her, and she hoped they'd reciprocated that to him in coping with his loss of Nadua.

****

Winnie drove a short distance before pulling into a parking lot in front of a museum. The sign in front of the building indicated that it provided a look into the history of the Prince William Sound. Lorelei's spirits lit up, as Chenega was a part of that very area. She brimmed with anticipation, until she and Winnie noted the empty lot. Given their early arrival, she hoped the museum simply hadn't opened yet.

Winnie consulted her phone to determine the hours of operation, but her sigh signaled bad news. "Well, they used to open on Sundays, but I guess they don't anymore. I'm sorry I didn't pay attention to that when I researched the schedule last night."

"No worries," Lorelei replied. "You've given me plenty of material as it is. If you want to head back up north, I wouldn't be disappointed in the least."

Winnie's fingertips tapped on the steering wheel. "I have connections with another small museum, but it would add a couple more hours to our trip. I just hated to keep you out so long. If you're up for it, though, I'd be happy to take you."

"I'm all in, as long as you have the time in your schedule."

Winnie nodded in agreement and made a phone call to the owner of the place. From the little she could ascertain, Lorelei learned the museum wasn't typically open, not only on a Sunday, but at this time of year at all. It seemed to cater to tourists who visited in the summertime, so the owner had to shovel the snow that piled up in front of the entrance during the months since it closed. Lorelei's manners deterred her from interrupting the conversation, but she wished she'd realized the inconvenience she was putting on the man when she expressed her desire to go.

She kept quiet until Winnie ended the call, after which she told her, "I'm sorry if your friend is going to a lot of trouble to accommodate me."

Winnie waved her hand dismissively. "It's no big deal. My brother is the owner, and he didn't have much to do today anyhow. Plus, he always likes to check on the building once a month or so through the off-season."

Lorelei's adrenaline surged. At last, Winnie mentioned her brother and even arranged for them to meet up with him. Should Lorelei pounce on the opportunity to inquire his name, or should she let it arise naturally? She'd have to learn it sooner or later, wouldn't she?

For the moment, she opted to remain casual and lead up to it. "So, are you both history buffs?"

"I have more of an instinctive curiosity about it than he used to, but he's grown into it, to a degree. The museum is his retirement job. A few years back, the previous owner fell into some financial trouble and was going to have to close it. He was a family friend, and we used to help him out when we were kids. Once we heard he would have to give it up, I couldn't let the museum collapse altogether. Even though I couldn't move out here to run it myself, I persuaded my brother to buy it with me and take care of operations when we have it open during summer. He enjoys it and has developed more of an interest in history like I did during my childhood. He's done a lot more improvements to it than I expected him to."

Lorelei grinned. "I look forward to meeting him."

"I'll probably let him give you the tour while I run over to check on my mom. She's recovering from some health challenges, so I've been going home pretty frequently this month. Truth be told, that's why I didn't put this on the original agenda. I knew that if I was in the area, I'd better go over there. I don't normally mind, but I didn't want to drag you into my personal obligations."

"It's no trouble to me. I completely understand your position, given what I'm going through with my uncle."

Winnie nodded, somber. "Isn't it sad to watch their health decline? My mom has never been an ill person. She always managed her health and ours in a homeopathic way, especially because of our culture. As the maladies of old age have crept up, though, she's had to resort to modern medicine."

"It catches up to all of us."

Winnie murmured an agreement before changing the subject. "Did you say your uncle was a photojournalist, too? Is that what inspired you to go into the field?"

"Yes, it did. From a young age, I loved to tinker with his camera and lenses, and he set up his own darkroom at home, which fascinated me. He'd never let me go in there when I was little because of the chemicals and equipment, so he thought I was just attracted to the forbidden, intrigue element of it. Once he allowed me entry when I turned nine, though, I couldn't get enough of studying the process. It became cathartic, and my science grades even improved due to the perspective it gave me on chemical reactions and the like."

"Wow. It's neat when interests grab us so early in life. I wish my girls experienced that, but nothing has stood out so far. They have time," she replied. "Was your uncle a freelancer, as well?"

"He started out that way, but within a couple of years, he craved some stability," Lorelei told her. "He settled down in Arizona, where my grandparents raised him and my dad, and he took a job with the small local press there. He used to tease me that I'd grow tired of the traveling and hustle, but I didn't. I'm getting the idea he wanted a bit more of a prestigious career than he let on, though, at least for a time."

"How do you gather that?"

Winnie's question surprised her, but she didn't find any harm in revealing the truth. "Not long ago, I learned he visited here after the earthquake, with the intent of writing an article to submit to renowned journals. He had his sights on winning an award."

"Really? What was his name? I might've come across it in my studies."

Lorelei chuckled inside, realizing she landed in the same trap she set with Doli. "He actually never published it. His trip showed him the toll of the tragedy, and I think he didn't want to use it for personal gain when so many were suffering. Plus, my parents died while he was here, so taking us on shifted his priorities."

"He sounds like a wonderful man."

Lorelei smiled. "He is."

"You should hit it off pretty well with my brother, Mack. He's always had a knack for photography, too. He didn't take it up professionally but has devoted more time to it since he retired."

Lorelei's endorphins twinkled throughout her being, with the remark serving as the conclusive proof she needed to connect this Mack with the one she met at the airport. Again, she grappled with whether or not to address their prior encounter. On the one hand, she didn't consider it very uncommon to link relations together, as people did so on a regular basis. In this case, however, she barely made acquaintance with either of them and her logic—if she dared to explain it all—may still seem like she'd given Mack a bit too much thought…which, in truth, she couldn't dispute.

She resolved to stay quiet, figuring Mack would recognize her when Winnie introduced them, ushering in a more casual way to reveal their recent history. Nonetheless, she had trouble pondering anything beyond their imminent reunion, embarrassed by her reawakened giddiness. She endeavored to keep tight reins on her glee, especially around Mack. As much as she worried over resembling a stalker to Winnie, she'd shudder with humiliation if she conveyed as much to him.

Plus, there must be a chance of another photographer named Mack with a daughter named Halyn and a new grandson named Ahanu, right?

To maintain the proper mindset, Lorelei returned the subject of conversation to the earthquake, filling in some of the gaps that her research hadn't addressed. She also asked more questions about the recovery process and how long it really took for the victims to settle back into a normal way of life. Winnie initially gave her insights from a historical perspective, relating facts about how many years it took to get certain infrastructure repaired and running again. After that, she added some of her personal experience.

"Being born in the aftermath of it, I can't claim that I understood how disrupted our world was. My mom didn't complain about the inconveniences we had to deal with, and she never let me see her mourn what we lost. My uncle was a father figure to Mack and me, much like yours was, so I didn't feel like my family was deficient in any way. Since most of my peers and classmates suffered similar losses and pretty much grew up under the same conditions, no one pointed out our challenges. We all considered everything around us as normal, for the most part. I'm almost ashamed to admit that I don't remember discussing my father with my mom until my late teens."

"I get that," Lorelei replied. "Even now, my uncle, brother, and I don't talk much about the fire that took our parents. We've had conversations about different memories, but it took a while to get to that point. I think Uncle Reed had to figure out the right balance of keeping them in our lives without reminding us of how much we missed them."

"I can only imagine," Winnie murmured. "I didn't appreciate what Mom underwent until I was pregnant. It didn't hit me so much with my first baby, given everything else that runs through your mind as a new mother, but with my second, I couldn't help but envision myself in her situation. My girls are spaced apart by just about the same length as my brother and I are, so that probably triggered my recognition. I still can't fathom how she stayed so strong while she managed a toddler and newborn with nothing to her name."

"That's incredible." Lorelei ruminated over how closely Winnie's mom's account mirrored that of Doli's mother and Nadua. She wondered how many expectant mothers there were when the earthquake struck. She pictured how neat it'd be to gather all of the babies born that year for her story but doubted she could pull off such a feat in her short time that remained. After a moment of consideration, she inquired, "Did your family know Doli Kuliktana before she worked for the historical society? Her mother had a baby soon after the quake, too."

"I met Doli through work, but I didn't know her outside of that. She never mentioned her mom to me. I'll have to ask her about it sometime."

She opened her mouth to ask if their family remembered Nadua, but they ran into a flurry of snow, making it imperative that Winnie focus on her driving. Again, Lorelei winced with guilt and a bit of trepidation over prompting her to continue the journey, but the adept driver didn't seem fazed. Still, Lorelei remained mute for much of the last leg of the trip.

She used the solitude to take in the views of the landscapes around them, realizing she hadn't taken advantage of many opportunities after her first day there. The one regret she had about her travels was the fact that she often had tunnel vision in her pursuit of her stories. At times, she didn't recall some of the areas she had gone to when she reexamined her passport and itineraries. Peering out the window, she took in scene after scene that could have been featured on a postcard. With their route taking them farther into the country, miles of untouched snow blanketed mountains and evergreen trees. The occasional small town offered variety to the trip and enhanced the idyllic appearance. The sights captivated her so much so that the notion of grabbing her camera didn't even occur to her, similar to her wonder over the Aurora when they landed.

Winnie exited the freeway and merged onto a road called Hope Highway, with the snow pretty much abating altogether. Having passed a town named Sunrise, Lorelei chuckled over the statewide optimism. "Whoever founded these places must've had a cheery demeanor."

"Hope actually dates back to the gold rush in the late 1800s. A miner discovered nuggets in Resurrection Creek, which made other prospectors flock to the area," the historian reported. "Rumor has it the settlers of the village of Hope named it after a young prospector, Percy Hope, but either way, it embodied the spirit of enthusiasm that prevailed during the era. We have a section of the museum devoted to it."

"Hope is your hometown?"

Winnie nodded. "We moved there when I was in my early teens. My mom had a variety of reasons for choosing it, but the name didn't hurt. After everything we'd gone through, we could use some hope, and the place didn't disappoint. Sure, we still had our share of challenges, but I'd say it was where we all began to live, not just exist. As I said before, I didn't deem anything about my childhood insufficient, but after we relocated, our family as a whole revived in a way I never realized we needed to. My mom, especially, grew into this different person."

"May I ask if she ever remarried?"

"Nope, she didn't. We never discussed it, but I've concluded that was a major contributor to her transformation. In retrospect, I think she felt the pressure from our tribe to reestablish a homeland and continue our life the way she originally planned, but we just couldn't. My dad was gone, along with everything we owned. Even if we lived in the same area, we couldn't live the same life. Once we came to Hope, we made a new beginning, instead of trying to begin the old again."

Lorelei could relate to the remark, long having believed she and Harley adjusted better to life without their parents by being away from their childhood home in Boston. Though she remembered the fear that the unfamiliar surroundings gave her during the first few months in Sedona, she settled down once they all established a routine. She couldn't fathom making that transition if she'd been around all of the reminders of her mom and dad.

Not wanting to make everything about her own history, she didn't share any of that with Winnie. Rather, she continued to take in the beautiful sights of the meandering highway, catching glimpses of moose and caribou on the edges of forests and lakes.

"Do you ever get used to seeing such majestic creatures all around you?"

Winnie nodded with an ashamed frown. "We do tend to take them for granted, unless we have the misfortune of hitting one on the road. Then, we gain a newfound appreciation for them, but it's not the kind you have right now."

Lorelei snickered. Within a few more minutes, Winnie turned off the highway onto an older road, landing them in a desolate-looking little town. Spotting the old-fashioned cabins and buildings, she felt like one of the characters in her nephews' favorite movie, who found himself lost in a forgotten burg. They drove a mile farther, and she had to wonder if they'd journeyed through a time portal that opened to pioneer days, complete with old barns and farm equipment. Impressing her still more, the arch ahead of them read *Hope and Sunrise Historical Museum*.

"This is your museum?" She gazed around the property that was set up like an early-twentieth-century village. A nearby sign directed visitors to a schoolhouse, blacksmith shop, and bunkhouse, among other attractions. "This is an immersive experience."

Winnie grinned and switched off the ignition. "We do our best to acquaint tourists with our heritage. I wish you could've toured it during the season. We won't be able to take you inside many of the buildings."

Lorelei winked. "I may just have to come back in a few months."

The two stepped out of the car, and Winnie pointed toward the front cabins, explaining that one was used as a guardhouse and another served as a place for modern visitors to pan for gold. With everything cloaked in snow, she couldn't make out many of the landmarks Winnie neglected to describe, but she could envision the picturesque setting it must make during summertime. Even now, she couldn't resist snapping some shots for her own collection.

A lone set of footprints led to the cabin that served as the museum building, so she and Winnie followed them. Lorelei took a glance at where the man's tracks began, with her sights closing in on a silver truck she'd ridden in her first morning in Alaska. Just the same, her breath caught in her throat the instant Mack emerged from the doorway, scattering ice-melt around the entrance.

His head remained downward while he performed the chore, his pace and movements rather harried. "I'm sorry, guys, but Mom sidelined me for longer than I anticipated."

"Is she okay?" Winnie questioned, snapping right into protective daughter mode.

"Yes." His unguarded, slightly miffed tone amused Lorelei. "Once I told her you were dropping by, she insisted I straighten up her place in case you brought your company over."

"Sorry about that. I doubt we'll have much time to visit if we want to get back to Anchorage at a reasonable hour. I figured I'd run over while you give Lorelei the tour."

He seemed ready to make a counterpoint, but the mention of Lorelei made him stop and whip his head upright. "Lorelei?"

Chapter Ten

Winnie's gaze swiveled between Mack and Lorelei. "Seems like I don't need to introduce you two."

Lorelei felt her cheeks heat up, even though she was more prepared for this encounter than Mack. "We took the same flight from Phoenix."

She almost added that they'd shared the same hotel but quickly realized how that could sound. Unaware of the kind of bond he had with his sister, she didn't want to overstep and cause any unneeded embarrassment. Rather, she opted to let him fill Winnie in on the rest.

He shifted his weight from one side to the other, appearing to debate his follow-up, until he said, "Yeah, if it wasn't for Lorelei, I would've lost Ahanu's pictures. My camera fell out of my bag in the terminal waiting area, and she spotted it."

"I figured you two would get along, both being shutterbugs," Winnie replied. Lorelei may not have known her very well, but she detected the mischievous intonation in her voice, especially after she continued with, "My mom will want to meet you for sure now. Every time I've talked to her since Mack made it home, all she can do is gush over those baby photos."

"Didn't you just say you probably wouldn't be able to stick around too long?"

"I reckon we can, so long as we all get moving. I'll take off, and you guys can catch up, on our history, that is."

Nobody could deny her impish demeanor there, so Lorelei and Mack shared a grin. He shook his head. "No matter how old we age, she's always ready to bust my chops somehow."

Lorelei laughed. "Speaking as a younger sister, I get it."

"I suppose it's my own fault for not connecting the dots when she mentioned having a reporter who was doing a story on the earthquake."

"How could you add it up? Anchorage is teeming with us right now."

His smirk signaled that he picked up on her sarcasm. She refrained from admitting the trail she'd followed all weekend to discern if he'd end up being Winnie's brother. She didn't want to tip him off about how much residence he'd taken up in her mind.

He led her into the building, saying, "Excuse the dust. We didn't expect visitors for another couple of months."

"No problem. Winnie mentioned that you aren't normally open right now. I appreciate you going to the trouble for me."

"It's all right. I was due for a checkup. Truth be told, I thought about offering this the other day, but we have very few artifacts from the earthquake. The one in Whittier has a better exhibit, but Winnie said it was closed today."

Lorelei nodded, suppressing her newfound glee over the development. After all, if the place hadn't been closed, they wouldn't have ventured down to Hope.

Trekking inside, Lorelei perused the menagerie of antiques that represented the early days in Hope and

Sunrise, like the rest of the village outside. Old tools hung on the walls alongside paintings, newspaper clippings, and hunting gear, with a corner devoted to animal hides and traps. Display cases held an array of household items, including bottles, coffee cans, and dish-wear, and Mack pointed out a few that had survived the earthquake. As they meandered around the single room, the displays advanced in the territory's history, encompassing the gold rush and onward.

Without much separation between the exhibits, the place reminded her more of an antique shop than a museum. Her facial expression must've conveyed her contemplation, prompting Mack to comment, "Some may term this hoarding, but we call it storytelling."

"I agree. Not long ago, I came across something at my uncle's house that anybody—including me—would've normally tossed, but it carried quite a message." *Which she yearned to fully decipher.*

He appeared to appreciate her words, even if he didn't proffer her the chance to elaborate. Still, she sensed his discomfort, maybe doubtful she'd consider the ordinary selection very interesting. To put him at ease, she asked questions regarding the variety of tales he recounted about the pioneers and their families. Her attempts seemed to work, as his posture relaxed, and his narratives grew more fluid. Though she couldn't use much of it for her article, she embraced the opportunity to spend more time with him and the insight it gave into his daily routine.

In many ways, the simplicity of the collection warmed her spirits. When she was younger, she may have deemed it boring, but now, she appreciated the window into the lifestyle people had back then. In the modern world, everyone depended on external sources for pleasure, but the selection here revealed that families made their own happiness. She noted the record player and piano in one area, as well as the books scattered about, and figured those were the main sources of entertainment the people didn't supply on their own.

Toward the end of the circle they made around the room, Mack showed her the original post office boxes the town had, complete with the recipients' names. After listening to his discourse, she spotted a counter with souvenirs they sold tourists and decided to buy a few mementos. Besides her desire to compensate him and Winnie for accommodating her, she didn't want to forget this afternoon with Mack.

When she slipped out her wallet and related her wish to make a purchase, he let out a guffaw. "I wouldn't take an elite world traveler like you as a sucker for tourist traps."

"And I wouldn't take a gentleman like you as one to heckle your guests," she retorted. "I guess we both learned something about each other."

After examining the assortment of shirts, postcards, and coffee mugs, she selected a mug for Uncle Reed, having picked up one for him from many of her trips, and bought herself a sweatshirt and pack of postcards.

As she studied one of the postcards that had a winter scene of the glaciers in the area, she had to ask him, "Did you take any of these gorgeous shots?"

"None of the ones you have are mine, but there is one here."

He rotated the carousel that displayed the selection and picked out one that showed an autumn landscape of a forest. Lorelei marveled again at his talent and the way he captured the shadows and colors at just the ideal angle. Her trained eye didn't detect an overuse of filters, either. It'd been a long time since she observed such skills in an amateur.

She handed him more money. "I'd like this one, too, please."

He waved her off. "It's on the house. I appreciate the nudge you gave me to get in here this month."

She fished out another dollar and handed it over, insistent. "Take it from a fellow freelancer: Accept the payment whenever you can."

He took it with a gracious smile. Since he hadn't shoveled around the rest of the village, she assumed he wouldn't extend the tour beyond the museum. To her surprise, he invited her outside, explaining he wanted to show her the old schoolhouse, which was the nearest cabin. With the snow over a foot deep, they crunched a path through it, and he offered her an arm a couple of times when she nearly sank into it. Meanwhile, he used the flashlight he carried to illuminate the dusky surroundings and shared details about some of the other buildings. He highlighted how everything ran when they were open during the summer. Despite the chill, she craved the hand-dipped ice cream served at one of the nearby booths.

Given the fact that they typically heated the schoolhouse with the potbelly stove in the corner, he warned her it wouldn't be warm inside. While he unlocked the door, she gloved back up like she should've done before they exited the building. She paid partial attention to his comments about the ongoing possibility of critters taking refuge in the cabins. She followed him through the door, and after he flipped on the lights, his body jerked before he released a gasp.

"I've always worried this would happen!"

Startled, she spun her head toward the area where he pointed, beholding a small bed that held two furry occupants. When her gaze landed on the bears' heads, she bolted for the door behind her, but her haste blinded her to the railing all around the entrance. Backing into it, she lost her footing and would've dropped to the floor if Mack hadn't extended his arm to steady her. They locked eyes for a moment, until his temples creased upward in the start of a grin.

Instead of being in a similar panic, he began to chuckle through his apology. "I'm so sorry! I must have improved my acting skills this winter."

"What do you mean?"

Alarming her, he approached the black bears and scooped up what proved to be just blankets made of skin. The attached heads and the pillows underneath them gave them the appearance of actual bodies, albeit being much smaller once the lenses of terror wore off.

Regardless of his apologetic nature, his smile didn't recede. "I pull this on all of our guests, but I've never garnered a reaction like that."

"Well, I guess I'm not only a patsy for tourist traps, but I'm a gullible sissy, too," she joked. "And you do more than heckle your patrons!"

He winked at her, and after a beat, he commenced his oratory about the building's history. "The first teacher opened it in the early 1900s, once young families settled here. With Alaska not being a recognized territory, they didn't have a required curriculum back then, but the early teachers recognized the subjects their students would need to make their own lives. After a bigger school was built, it became a regular house, and the man who owned it at the time weathered the earthquake inside of it."

With Mack's permission, Lorelei photographed the house from various angles, in awe of the detail preserved in the exhibit. Unlike the museum, the artifacts were neatly placed, creating the authenticity of a classic schoolhouse, with desks, books, and even a small chalkboard with the founding teacher's name written on it. More than that, a wooden frame wearing a suit and topped off with a smiling face paid further homage to the man. Completing the nostalgic ambiance, the design of the original wallpaper was duplicated and hung.

When Lorelei snapped enough shots, she and Mack set back out to the museum. With the wind picking up and a flurry whipping small snowflakes everywhere, they didn't linger to further discuss the village, which was already cloaked in darkness. They raced across the path as fast as they could without falling into the snow. Just before they made it to the museum's back door, it opened without assistance, startling Lorelei, though she didn't jump like she had when Mack fooled her about the bears.

An instant later, Winnie's head appeared behind the door. They quickened their pace even more to retreat into the heated cabin.

Winnie wore a grin, shifting to her brother. "I had a feeling you would take her out to meet Red and Herring!"

Lorelei couldn't suppress a giggle over what she guessed to be the bears' names, as Mack defended himself, "Well, the schoolhouse does have a connection to the earthquake."

"Uh huh," Winnie retorted, clearly unconvinced of his pure motives.

He leveled a dastardly but handsome grin at Lorelei. "She fell for it better than anyone ever has, which means you owe me fifty bucks."

"Don't pay him anything," Lorelei countered. "He also snookered me into buying souvenirs. He claimed he took a photo on one of the postcards, but I'm not sure I believe that anymore, either."

They shared a chuckle over the banter, until Mack questioned Winnie, "Are you guys going to take off for Anchorage now or stick around for a little while?"

"I need to consult Lorelei about that. Mom is actually feeling good enough to go to dinner and is trying to coax us all into going to the Seaview to eat together. As she reminded me, we will need to eat somewhere along the way, so we could grab a bite around here to save us a pit stop. I don't want to obligate you, Lorelei, if you would rather get back to your hotel sooner than not."

"I'm up for anything. I don't have special plans and would enjoy checking out a local eatery instead of fast food, along with meeting your mom."

Mack and Winnie seemed pleased with her agreement and hashed out their agenda to get their mother to the restaurant. Winnie suggested she could take Lorelei, while he returned to give their mom a lift. From their conversation, Lorelei gathered the older woman no longer had good balance, so Mack's strength made him better suited to accompany her. The siblings whispered something between themselves before they parted ways, making Lorelei uneasy.

She didn't pry into the exchange, with it none of her

business, but Winnie didn't make her wait long to learn the subject. "If you wouldn't mind, please don't discuss the earthquake with my mom. Like I told you earlier, she took so long to rebound from it, and it's still a sensitive topic. We avoid it as much as possible. I didn't even mention that your article was about it, and I don't think Mack let her know, either."

"I can appreciate that. No worries. The rest of this afternoon will be off the record," Lorelei assured her.

Winnie's posture relaxed. "Thank you. I realize I mentioned the possibility of putting you in touch with some relatives, but I haven't recruited anyone yet. My uncle may be up for it, but I haven't been able to get ahold of him so far."

Lorelei wondered if Mack had any recollection of it, but considering both his and Winnie's silence on his perspective, she gathered it was a sore subject. "Not a problem. You've more than done your part."

Since they'd have time to kill before Mack could get their mom out, she gave Lorelei a tour through the small town. She followed Mack's truck to their mother's house, where they'd lived since moving to Hope. The log cabin had a cottage style, with a porch around three sides and a swing by the front door, which Winnie's mom sat on every night when the weather allowed. Mack's place was just around the corner, but they didn't go by it since it was located on a dead-end street. They passed the school the siblings attended when they were adolescents, along with the grocery store they frequented, and both worked at before they graduated.

Heading back toward where they started, they ended up at the historic part of town, where most tourists visited. The old strip featured a community hall, coffee shop, and several stores, which like the museum, were only open during tourist season. Up ahead, an RV park overlooked Resurrection Creek, glistening under the surrounding glaciers. Once again, Lorelei wished she could experience the quaint area when it had more life.

Thankfully, their destination was one of the few businesses that remained open year-round. At first glance, the Seaview Café and Bar appeared to be two separate establishments, but inside, it was one combined space. Being a Sunday afternoon, it didn't bustle with much energy, but the stage in the bar area signaled that it was a venue for live music. Framed photos on the wood-paneled walls showed off the artists who'd performed there, most of whom were local singers, according to Winnie. Lorelei doubted the place catered to a very rowdy audience, with the tight knit community feel evident as soon as they entered the building. Before they could even sit down, the customers and staff alike engaged Winnie in conversation, inquiring about her and her family's wellbeing.

Of course, Lorelei garnered a lot of attention being the outsider, with everybody interested in who she was and what business she had in Hope. Because of Winnie's request to refrain from talking about the earthquake, she struggled with sharing much about her project, especially since the people displayed such curiosity. The journalist in her cringed over letting so many potential sources slip through her fingers, considering the majority seemed old enough to have survived it. She gave herself a break, though, in light of how much she'd accomplished that day alone. The least she could do for Winnie and Mack was to ensure their meal with their mom didn't have any hiccups.

She and Winnie ordered drinks and a plate of garlic bread for their appetizer while they waited for Mack to arrive with his mom. The owner acted as their server, and her face lit up when Winnie informed her that her mother was well enough to join them.

"Miss Azalea hasn't been in here since summertime! Do you think she'd feel up to her special dish? Hugh's had a batch since the fall that he's itching to share with her. We offered to bring some to the house for her, but she didn't have the appetite for it last time we called."

"She gave me special instructions to order it for her, Luna," Winnie affirmed. "I really appreciate you keeping in touch with her."

"No problem, sweetie. It's our pleasure. She was one of our most loyal customers from the time we took over the place. I'm sure she still would be if her circumstances allowed." Luna patted Winnie on the shoulder. She smiled toward Lorelei in a mischievous fashion. "Should we make up a plate for your friend?"

Winnie winked. "It depends. Have you ever heard of muktuk, Lorelei?"

"As a matter of fact, I have," Lorelei admitted, remembering Uncle Reed's wretched description. "My uncle tried some when he visited. He wasn't a fan."

Luna snickered. "Most newcomers aren't. It's an acquired taste. Would you like to give it a try?"

The women's daring smiles put pressure on her. Intimidated, she shrugged. "I wouldn't mind having a bite, but I don't want to take it away from the ones who really enjoy it."

They teased her about her gracious excuse, before Luna returned to the kitchen. Lorelei consulted the menu. "I don't even see muktuk listed on here."

"It isn't. Luna and her husband hit it off with Mom when they bought the Seaview, and they learned she enjoyed it as much as they did. It was more common in Chenega than it is here, so they don't feature it for anyone but her."

"She sounds like a special lady."

"I can't disagree. Speaking of which…"

Winnie motioned toward the entrance, where Mack was escorting a shorter woman. Bundled up in a coat made of deer skin, she wore a matching scarf and hat along with knitted mittens. The apparel reinforced the notion Lorelei inferred that she hadn't strayed much from home. As she approached, Lorelei could recognize the features she shared with her children, with her eyes shaped like Winnie's while her son inherited her nose. Though her skin had a dark tone like theirs, it seemed pretty sunken in and lacked pigment. Lorelei realized that happened with age, but all things considered, she believed the poor woman had suffered a bout of illness.

Her kids helped her out of the winter gear, but they left her hat atop her head without question. No tendrils of hair peeked out from underneath the cap. Based off her dealings with Gabe's wife, Clara, and other cancer patients, she deduced Azalea was fighting the terrible disease, but she wouldn't ask for confirmation. On the contrary, she maintained a cheery smile as Azalea took a seat.

Once settled, Azalea greeted her, "You must be the famous Lorelei."

Lorelei shook her hand. "I don't know about the famous part. Seems like you're the celebrity around here. Everybody's asked Winnie about you already, and I hear you even have your own dish nobody else can order."

Azalea cracked a grin. "It's just boring in our neck of the woods."

Her humility tickled Lorelei, especially when the ensuing minutes attested to her neighbors' affection for her. The younger trio sat, quiet, while Luna and other workers circled over one-by-one to converse with her, and the scattered diners took their turns, too. The majority kept their repartees casual and refrained from prying about her health, but the few she appeared close to like Luna drew her out more. From their discussions, Lorelei discerned Azalea had completed chemotherapy treatments for cancer that was found in a brain tumor the previous year. Fortunately, it was located in a region where surgeons were able to remove it.

Lorelei sensed Azalea's reluctance to disclose many personal details around a stranger, catching her glances across the table. Thus, she endeavored to busy herself with other activities, first pouring over the small menu with far greater scrutiny than it merited. Then, she resumed her examination of the restaurant's rustic décor, meandering to the windows that lined the bar portion, which overlooked a patio deck that probably opened during summer. Her heels tapped against the oak floorboards, and though she didn't don cowboy boots, she figured the floor had hosted plenty of line dances.

As she peered into the dark sky, another set of footsteps thumped toward her, and she shifted to find Mack at her side. They stood together in silence for a moment, but it didn't seem uncomfortable in the least. She didn't venture a guess about what he might have on his mind, but she supposed all of the talk about his mom's diagnosis had to take a toll on his spirits.

She focused on the positives of the community's

care. "Your mom clearly made an impact on your hometown. It's so touching to see how invested people are in her care. I'm sure it can be overwhelming at times, but it's becoming rarer and rarer that somebody cares about anyone but themselves, especially those of different generations."

He nodded. "When I visit my sister or my in-laws in Anchorage, I can't get over how unfamiliar they are with their own neighbors. Up there, a house can change hands three times before they even learn the owners' names. There's no way that would fly in this town."

"I believe that, and I haven't been around for more than two hours."

Mack pivoted to watch the scene at their table again, and his eyes shone with gratitude for his mom's reception. "Hope has been a nice balance for us. In many ways, it's reminiscent of a reservation, where everyone is a family. At the same time, though, she didn't face the same pressure the tribe put on her. Don't get me wrong, I'm proud of my heritage and upbringing, but everything is based on tradition and following our ancestry. With all that my mom has been through, she experienced how uncertain life can be and that you can't always fit your feet into everybody else's prints, so to speak."

"I can relate. Even in this day and age, people draw all sorts of conclusions about me and why I never married or settled down. In truth, I don't have much of a reason for it, other than not finding anyone fast enough to slow me down," she joked. "I didn't plan to be a rolling stone or convince myself I was a big fish in a small pond. I adore my uncle who raised me, and my brother's all right, too."

She paused, but his kind yet intrigued silence helped

175

her summon the strength to continue, "My parents died when their restaurant had a kitchen fire that consumed it. I was little, but one of my few memories is them both emphasizing that we'd run the place one day. Mom would let me stand by her at the hostess lectern and hand menus to patrons, and Dad let us help him put away some of the supplies. We were learning to take over the reins and had that concept of a legacy when we were so young, only to lose it all in one tragic night. Maybe that's why I never had a deep reverence for putting down roots, kind of like how your mom's views of tradition changed."

"Tragedies have a way of shaping a person. Winnie's probably told you how we lost our dad." He snuck a glance at Azalea, and Lorelei nodded with understanding. "It bonded my mom and me, so I reckon that's why I stayed put, other than the five years I spent in Seward with my wife after we were first married. I think the world needs a good mix of homebodies and nomads."

She giggled at his dryness. "Your perspective does evolve as you grow older. I've made a lot of acquaintances through the years, but I doubt any of them would show me a fraction of the concern your mom has received today. I'm not complaining, since I have to admit I've never extended that kind of regard for them, either. For the most part, we're all respectful of one another and have a level of admiration, but we just spin in an orbit like the planets, never getting very close."

"Don't go too hard on yourself. An uncaring person wouldn't pay any attention to a camera under an amateur photographer's seat, let alone have dinner at a hole-in-the-wall in the middle of nowhere with a strange family."

"After your cruel bear stunt, no less." She elbowed

him in jest. "Jokes aside, I admire the way you and Winnie are there for your mom. I may not know you well, but I can tell you've done right by her. I'm sorry for your struggles this past year."

He released a sigh. "Thank you. I can't claim that it never has its frustrating moments. On the occasions when I feel like I'm near my breaking point, I harken back to when Winnie and I both contracted chickenpox at the same time. I came down with it first and then shared it with her, and since she was on the young side to develop it, she suffered a worse case. With her immune system down, she also caught a flu-like bug, so we really had Mom running. Back then, I just threw myself a pity party and whined that she couldn't give me her exclusive attention, but years later, I grasped how devoted she was, even when she was no doubt at her wit's end. How can I not repay that?"

Lorelei agreed with him and reflected on her own intentions to provide for Uncle Reed. "That's what I keep telling my brother about our uncle. He halted his life for us at an age when most people are just picking up their stride. Of course, my brother holds it over me that he's been providing for him all this time, when I've been globetrotting in the name of my career. Maybe he's right. If he hadn't walloped me with a wakeup call by admitting him into a nursing home, I'm not sure I would've taken stock of my duty to him."

Mack surprised her by clutching her hand and giving it a squeeze. "What you would've done doesn't amount to anything. All that matters is what you're going to do."

Chapter Eleven

By the time Mack and Lorelei roamed back over to the table, Azalea had removed her hat. Lorelei surmised she either warmed up enough or was no longer uncomfortable showing her head, which only had short gray fuzz to cover it. Regardless, the woman had a lighter demeanor than when she first arrived, perhaps because of the gracious welcome she received.

The four of them munched on the garlic bread Winnie ordered and enjoyed easy companionship while they awaited their meals. Azalea seemed to soak up the chance she had to be with both of her children, who admitted that they typically take turns when caring for her and rarely get to visit. She gave the two of them much of her attention, listening to stories about Winnie's work and family as well as a couple of anecdotes Mack shared about his vacation in Arizona. They all included Lorelei in the conversation, never making her feel like the third wheel. From the way Azalea interacted with her own children, Lorelei gathered she simply wasn't the type of woman to pry into other people's affairs. Even so, her kind consideration of what they said showed how much she cared about them.

Given that she hadn't eaten any fish entrees during her stay, Lorelei reckoned she'd better do so while she had the opportunity to taste the Alaskan specialty. Thus, she ordered halibut, a favorite whenever she was in the mood for seafood. As she took her second slice of garlic bread, she had to smile inside, imagining the combination of garlic and fish on her breath. She didn't anticipate Mack offering a kiss that evening, but she still made sure to dig out her breath mints.

Once Luna set down the platter of muktuk, however, Lorelei shut down any notions of even sharing a peck with anybody at the table. In her mind, her uncle's portrayal of the dish didn't do it justice. Even without a clue of its taste, its appearance alone threatened her appetite. Its white exterior seemed to have a rubbery texture and had gray tones running through it, reminding her of fake eyeballs. Thankfully, the dish didn't have a strong odor, at least from afar, enabling her to remain pretty poker faced. That served her well, with the family's curious gazes piercing through her.

Azalea's impish grin revealed her sense of humor. "We should let our guest have first dibs."

"Like I told Luna, I don't want to take any away from you guys. It sounds like this is a pretty special treat."

"See how cordial she is," Mack taunted.

"There's no greater treat than watching someone experience muktuk for the first time," Azalea added.

Lorelei leaned back in her chair, crossing her arms. "I'm starting to understand how people in small towns like this find entertainment: They wait for unsuspecting visitors to arrive so they can fool them about local culture."

Azalea winked. "Give us a break. We usually go all winter without tourists. We need to maximize our amusement with you to hold us over for three more months."

Lorelei couldn't hide her own delight over the predicament. She elected to humor them, sticking out her hand to pick up a piece of the meat. The texture met her expectations, but she didn't anticipate it being unheated. Despite her better judgement, she whispered to them, "Shouldn't it be warmer?"

"We prefer it raw," Winnie replied with a smirk.

"Is this another 'Red and Herring' prank?" she questioned. "No hard feelings, but I don't deem salmonella poisoning as all that comical."

"Just to prove that it's safe, we'll start without you," Azalea told her.

Lorelei didn't argue, wishing they'd gobble up the dish without her having to taste a morsel. Her manners, however, compelled her to take the piece she'd already touched. She placed it on the corner of her plate, content she could at least enjoy her meal before following through with the veiled dare. On the other hand, she hoped having it afterward wouldn't cause her meal to make an emergency evacuation.

The trio made a big show of how much they relished their dinner, smacking their lips together and exchanging remarks about the quality of it. Whether the trio took more pleasure in the muktuk or the opportunity to needle her about it, Lorelei couldn't say for sure. She figured they gleaned much satisfaction from both. Even so, she didn't call them out over it, nor did they goad her about taking the long-awaited bite. Just the same, she continued to sense their anticipation, catching their sly glances at the piece she'd claimed.

Azalea temporarily shifted everyone's focus from the game when she inquired of Lorelei, "Are you writing an article about small towns?"

In mid-chew, she appreciated having a moment to consider how she would phrase her words, with Mack and Winnie leveling cautious gazes in her direction. She couldn't give her the same line she offered her uncle about it concerning natural disasters in general, seeing as it would reveal the exact matter that they wanted to avoid. Moreover, she generalized the subject even further. "It involves several different areas. It's a human-interest story on how people adapt to various circumstances. I enjoyed learning about the gold rush here and how they had to establish the school, without guidelines, no less."

Mack awarded her with a discreet thumbs-up across the table.

To their gratitude, Azalea accepted the vague explanation, and Lorelei tried to compensate by relating some of her experiences from other assignments. Before long, however, the attention circled back to the muktuk in front of her. With her plate almost empty of her fish and fries, she couldn't delay the inevitable anymore. In all honesty, she was full, but she didn't suspect the Holts would let her off that easy.

She sipped her soda to clear her palate but made sure to leave an adequate amount for the same purpose afterward. Picking the meat up again, she still cringed at the texture and temperature, not to speak of the raw notion. She did her best to discard all of those elements from her mind as she drew it closer. "Here we go."

The three of them beheld her as if they were sitting in a movie theater, and she noted Luna along with a few other diners halt their own activities to observe her. During her first couple of chews, she didn't deem it worth the hype she'd partly caused, having tasted worse elsewhere. The chewiness of it surprised her, with it reminding her a bit of chewing gum…albeit without the fruity or minty sweetness. She'd classify it as savory on that spectrum, and Uncle Reed's narrative about the flavor's different phases rang in her head the further she progressed. She detected hints that tasted similar to oysters—not among her favorite foods—but the oiliness alone overwhelmed her. Despite her attempts not to let her face contort in disgust, the glints of humor in everybody else's eyes signaled that her lackluster opinion of it showed.

Luna broke the ice. "I have another batch in the freezer if you would care for a bigger helping."

The comment sent them all into cackles, including Lorelei. Once she swallowed, she guzzled the rest of her drink like she predicted she would need to. She continued to perceive her audience's anticipation for her to voice her thoughts. In the end, she settled on a wry takeaway. "I'll agree that it's an acquired taste."

More laughter ensued, before one of the local men declared, "We ought to have that printed on a shirt by now!"

The group granted her a round of applause, clearly relishing the interaction with the tourist. Recalling the latter part of Uncle Reed's account, she murmured, "Now, I need to try some thimbleberry jam."

"I could go for that, too," Winnie agreed.

"Well, I don't have any of that, but would a brownie on the house suffice for you four?" Luna proposed.

Nobody hesitated to acquiesce, and the generous owner even heated up the desserts. While they chowed down on the treat, they swapped tales about introducing muktuk to others. Though Alaska natives, Mack's wife and Winnie's husband hadn't partaken of it before marrying into the family, and neither one developed more than a tolerance for it. Observing their elation in reliving the memories, Lorelei brimmed with joy over how the afternoon unfolded. It may not have afforded her loads of research material, but it warmed her heart to be surrounded by that much love, especially in view of the adversity they'd underwent.

They polished off their sweets pretty quickly, after which Winnie and Lorelei shared an understanding look that they needed to retreat back north. Judging by her somber eyes, Lorelei could tell she wasn't eager to depart any more than Lorelei. Truth be told, Lorelei had an even harder time parting from Mack than she did when he dropped her off at the airport. From the moment they met in Phoenix, an invisible pull seemed to connect them, and their time together at the museum and dinner reinforced it, at least to her. That said, she still didn't have the confidence to tackle the subject of continuing the relationship.

Mack and Winnie cooperated to help get Azalea ready to brave the cold again, so Lorelei decided to assist by warming up both vehicles. Mack handed her the keys to his truck, so she started his ignition first in order for the cabin to be as toasty as possible for Azalea. Right after she revved up her rental, her phone began ringing, and the ID announced that it was Uncle Reed. Because of the darkness, she worried over why he would be calling so late, but her clock reminded her of how early it was, even with the time difference.

"Hey, you," she greeted him. "How has your weekend been?"

"Probably not as exciting as yours, but we've gone

all day without having to send for the ambulance. That counts for something."

She snickered. "It does, especially when you don't have a need, either."

"I save my medical emergencies for when you're around," he teased. "Nobody else pays me that kind of attention."

"Thank you, I guess?"

"All kidding aside, how's your story coming along?" Uncle Reed asked.

"Pretty well. I've compiled enough research now to be able to afford some personal time up here."

"Don't get too cocky now. You know how deceiving it can be to have all of these sources and then learn they gave you phony reports."

He'd drilled the caveat into her since her days of being an intern at Mountainscape News. She used to respond with an exasperated *I know*, but in her older years, she recognized his need to feel useful. "Very true. As sad as the subject matter may be, I've enjoyed the people I've met and the underlying message of resilience. It's refreshing after the serious pieces I've done, especially during the election cycle."

"Canadians are pretty polite and probably trustworthy, for the most part," he replied, which helped put her in the right frame of mind so that she could keep up her little ruse. His next sentence endangered it altogether, though. "Did you ever accept that assignment about the commemoration of the earthquake in Alaska?"

Since he never brought it up after his unusual episode at the nursing home, Lorelei assumed he'd forgotten it, especially with all that happened in the following days. Under pressure, she gripped the steering wheel in front of her like she was driving through Los Angeles at rush hour. "That's actually the brunt of my story right now. I've been in Anchorage the past couple of days."

"The people up there are friendly, too."

His quiet, solemn voice melted and crushed her heart all at once, and she wondered if he even meant for her to hear the remark. She debated how to reply, weighing whether or not to seize the chance to draw him out. Under normal conditions, she would quiz him on his experience, but because of what she discovered, she concluded it would be a step into restricted territory. At last, she latched onto a compromise. "They sure are. Although they have strange tastes in food. Have you ever heard of a dish called muktuk?"

"Boy, have I," he confirmed, and his tone indicated his smile, but he didn't elaborate.

Undeterred, Lorelei continued, "I think the whale had better use for it than we do!"

Uncle Reed chuckled. "From my standpoint, I believe you're right."

She mustered the nerve to press farther. "Did you get to try it?"

"Just once, a long time ago," he confessed. "Maybe I'll tell you about it someday, and we can compare notes."

"I wish you would," she replied, meaning it more than he realized.

****

Lorelei wrapped up her conversation with Uncle Reed, unsure of how much longer the Holts would take to emerge from the restaurant. She exited the car and paced back toward the café, spotting Mack and Winnie ushering out their mom. Lorelei stood in place to keep from getting in their way, but she hollered a warning that the ramp had a few slick patches due to the freshly fallen snow. Though salt pellets proved the staff had scattered ice-melt earlier, the path needed another application.

The three navigated the treacherous areas slowly but efficiently, and Lorelei relaxed enough to contemplate the goodbye she'd give Mack. Just like at the airport, she figured she wouldn't meet up with him again, but the circumstances didn't permit a lengthy farewell. Besides, she couldn't predict if he reciprocated her desire for more time together. With all of the variables at play, she kept in mind that they had each other's contact information, so the send-off didn't have to be final in the fullest sense.

Maybe she could arrange another story about The Last Frontier eventually.

As she entertained the prospect, the family had finally made it up to her, and she told Azalea, "It's a pleasure to meet you, Ms. Holt. I'm thrilled by the coincidences that led me to all of you. You're special people, and I hope things continue to improve for you."

"Thank you, Lorelei. I wish we could've spent more time together, but even in this short span, I think I have the full picture of how delightful you are—pun intended."

Lorelei beamed over the wit she possessed woven into her serious persona. She couldn't ascertain if the mother was hinting at her son's impression of her, and without good lighting, Mack's face didn't allude to anything, either. Hence, she refused to jump to any conclusions and interpreted it to be a clever quip.

They accompanied her straight up to the passenger's

seat, and Winnie opened the door for her. Azalea raised her left leg to climb into the cab, and despite Mack's guiding hand to steady her, her right foot slid out from under her, causing her to fall into him. The strong man maintained his balance, but Winnie sped around to render assistance, followed by Lorelei. Between the three of them, they managed to lift her into the seat, but the woman's groans of pain and inability to move her right leg provided no reassurance of it being a mere slip.

Lorelei scrutinized the ground for an icy glaze that triggered the incident, but the parking spot remained dry. Mack and Winnie's attempts to get her to answer their frantic questions were met with muffled responses, conjuring up the fresh memories of Uncle Reed's akinesia episode.

Unlike him, however, Azalea didn't wear a glossy stare, but her furrowed brow and agonized expression revealed her intense pain. She muttered, "My side."

"What do you mean by your side, Mom?" Mack asked. "Your leg, your foot, or what?"

"My side," Azalea repeated.

"We should get her to the clinic," Winnie declared.

"Would you like me to call 9-1-1?" Lorelei offered.

Mack shook his head. "We don't have any ambulances or hospitals nearby. Our only choice is to find out if Dr. McHenry can see her tonight. If he isn't available, we'll have to decide whether to get her to another clinic or hike up to Anchorage."

Winnie agreed with him and told him she'd run back to Azalea's house to retrieve her file of various medical information. While she drove, her trembling hands exposed her anxiety over her mom's condition. She confided a few of her fears in Lorelei. "Maybe some of the ice stuck to her boot and made her slip. Because of what she's been through, though, I'm so afraid it's another tumor or a different neurological cause. With her complaints about her side, the possibility of a stroke seems likely, as well."

Lorelei had similar wonderings, but she withheld them. "At least her speech didn't sound slurred. One of my other uncles suffered one a while back, and his kids could barely understand him."

Winnie nodded, appearing grateful for the input, but she continued spiraling through her quandary. "I just hope we didn't bring this on by taking her out. Her doctors cautioned us that she needed to stay close to home during winter because of the cold, germs, and whatnot, and she has. That's why I took pity on her today; she was getting cabin fever, and I could tell she felt left out of the chance to meet you."

Lorelei patted her arm resting on the console between them. "Observing you guys interact over dinner enriched me more than anything I've witnessed in a long time…even if part of your enjoyment came at my expense! I'm sure it fulfilled her, too, and I doubt she'd trade your companionship for anything, no matter what."

****

When Winnie made the pit-stop to collect Azalea's medications and insurance documents, she invited Lorelei to take a restroom break so they wouldn't have to stop again. Lorelei took advantage of it but tried not to delay the process. By the time she finished, Winnie had received word from Mack that Azalea's doctor was able to meet them at his clinic.

"The downside is he can't run any tests that would determine if she had a stroke, but at least he can check her vitals and do an X-ray to learn if she broke a bone," Winnie informed Lorelei. "I think I'm going to pack up a few extra supplies in case we're in for an overnight hospital stay. I'm sorry to delay our trip back."

"Don't worry on my account. I don't have to be back in Anchorage tonight if you don't. It's no trouble if you would like to stick around. I could come along or get a hotel room to spend the night."

"Or you could head back without me, and Mack or my husband could drive me home whenever we know what's going on. If Mom is transferred to the hospital, we'll all be making the trip, anyhow."

"That's not necessary, as far as I'm concerned. If you need to stay past tomorrow, we could talk about that, but I'm happy to help out however I can for now."

Winnie paused to mull it over, until she suggested, "Why don't you stay here, at least while we're at the clinic? We don't have many nice hotels around here, and I hate to see you have to camp out in an uncomfortable waiting room. It's bad enough when you're forced to for your own family."

Lorelei accepted the invitation, happy to accommodate them and provide them with some privacy. Nonetheless, she was surprised again by the trust Winnie showed in her, despite being a stranger. Sure, she would have Lorelei's rental car as collateral, but she still didn't consider it a very even trade. She had to wonder if Winnie felt the same inexplicable bond that Lorelei did with both her and Mack.

On her way out, Winnie pointed out where she could get drinks or a snack if she wished during her stay. She also welcomed her to use the television to pass the time. Lorelei snickered inside, finally getting a glimpse into

Karina Bartow

Winnie's maternal side while she rattled off the options in a frazzled manner.

After she departed, Lorelei continued to feel like an intruder in the homey living room. She admired the woman's old-fashioned style, noting how much it differed from the tourist spots where she'd spent most of her visit. Azalea paid homage to her heritage with several tapestries and carved trinkets, but she didn't showcase wildlife or much nature in general. In many ways, the interior would've fit in almost anywhere. The furnishings were dark wood yet modern, but every blanket in the ample stash of quilts that hung across the backs of the seats appeared homemade.

When she retrieved a glass of water, she noticed the stack of unwashed dishes on the counter. Out of sympathy for Mack and Winnie's heavy load, which would intensify if Azalea suffered a major injury, she resolved to wash them. Azalea hadn't modernized enough to upgrade to a dishwasher, so Lorelei located the soap and sponge while she filled up the sink. Even so, she wouldn't put anything except the cups away, uncomfortable rummaging into the cupboards Winnie didn't display to her.

As she dried off her hands, she marveled at the collage of family photos hanging on the wall behind the small dinner table. She stepped closer to study them better, finding most of them to feature Mack and Winnie. The collection didn't include many professional portraits, other than those taken at Mack's and Winnie's weddings. She took special note of Mack's bride, who resembled Halyn.

With photography on the brain, Lorelei decided to use the time to review her shots from the marathon day.

Recalling that her camera's battery indicator was flashing when she switched it off at the museum, she retrieved her backup pack before she powered it on. When she opened the pocket to do so, one of Uncle Reed's letters that she stuffed inside that morning popped out. The way it was folded pronounced that it was among the few she had yet to read. Without anything pressing on her agenda, she allowed it to distract her from her original task.

Gabe and Clara,

If you haven't begun the search for my replacement, consider this my two weeks' notice. I've arrived at the unequivocal decision to stay here with the family I've already made in my heart. Nadua never told me what to do with my future, but every time I envision leaving her and Makya, I'm crippled with misery. Not only am I distraught over her uncertain position without me, I can't imagine returning to a life without her.

I've lined up a job with a local paper, and we're investigating our housing prospects. We'll stay in the hotel until Nadua has the baby, which her midwife says could be within five weeks. I've taken over everything I can to make her as comfortable as possible, with one exception: I've asked her to marry me if she's so inclined. To my utter elation, she agreed to be my wife, so we're set to go to the judge Friday.

I plan to come to Sedona once the baby's born and everyone's settled so I can sell the house and haul the rest of my junk up here. Until then, my friends, I want you to know how much you mean to me. You gave me the stability I craved and impacted my professional as well as my personal development more than I can express. Maybe I can convey it to a degree, though, by telling you

Nadua and I have chosen to name our son Matto Gabriel or Winnie Clara for a daughter.

Like most of the other letters, Uncle Reed's words pelted Lorelei with astonishment, compassion, and wonder. When she read his announcement of their impending marriage, her gaze shifted up to the date, which—as she dreaded—occurred three days before her parents' tragic deaths. The blaze had happened on a Wednesday night, and she and Harley flew to Arizona on Saturday. Uncle Reed would've had to part from his wife-to-be mere hours ahead of their nuptials…and weeks, at most, before she'd deliver the child they'd named together.

Winnie Clara for a daughter.

The statement sent chills through Lorelei. Similar to her intrigue when Winnie mentioned Halyn and Ahanu at the library, she calculated the possibilities again and again of whether this could be the woman with whom she'd spent the day. With the name somewhat more common, she held back from becoming dogmatic. Plus, Winnie's mom went by Azalea Holt, not Nadua Macawi. And Mack…

…could've been short for Makya.

Her mind sought a way to determine the validity of her hunch. An instant later, her hands scrambled for the photo that sparked all of this. Buried deeper in the same pocket as the letters, she extracted it to compare to the pictures on the walls around her. With Makya so small in the ones she developed, she had difficulty getting a clear enough look to match him up to the older boy in the framed photos. Undeniably, though, the toddler bore a resemblance to Mack.

She peered around for a picture of a younger version

of Azalea, but she didn't spot any. She figured many, if not all, of the ones she may have had from her early years would have been destroyed in the tsunami. The youngest shot she found was taken at Mack's high school or college graduation, which would have occurred fifteen or twenty years after the one of Nadua and Uncle Reed. Mack's mother may not have had the same youthful skin or as round of a face as pregnant Nadua did, but her nose, smile, and quite a few other features were similar to the expectant woman.

Reeling from the alignment of plausible coincidences, Lorelei started to question whether she'd lost touch with reality. Might she be asleep on the flight to Anchorage, dreaming up these romantic twists of fate? Though she took this assignment wishing to figure out more about Nadua, she never would've fathomed having the opportunity to meet her and her children, let alone enter her home. Why would she? The odds had to be astronomical.

And yet, a tiny voice inside of her insisted she knew it all along.

Nonetheless, she ignored the whimsical voice. An email alert pinged her phone, so she checked it in an effort to ground herself back in the real world. The top pair of messages contained unneeded sales promotions, but she caught up on one from Cal and another business-related memo. After that, Mack's chain with her from the previous day appeared, and she was compelled to take a second gander at the attachments he sent. She admired the ones of the Northern Lights again, before she landed on the beautiful pose of Mack cradling Ahanu.

Without the time or reason to examine it in great detail yesterday, Lorelei hadn't paid much regard to the stuffed toy Mack held, aside from suspecting it to be a family heirloom. Tonight, however, she zoomed in on the animal, enabling that pesky, hopeful inner voice. True to her arguably delusional predictions, it was a moose. She dropped the phone on the coffee table in front of her and flipped through the pictures from the undeveloped film. She stopped at the one that first introduced her to Nadua and Makya, in which they stood among the rubble of their house.

She zeroed in on the stuffed animal in Makya's hand and couldn't dismiss her repressed convictions any longer. The handmade moose—which Uncle Reed also referenced in his account of meeting them—was the same one Mack gifted his baby grandson, meaning Mack was Makya.

And Azalea was the woman Uncle Reed loved.

Chapter Twelve

In the moments after Lorelei's epiphany, she struggled to figure out how to proceed. A plethora of urges surged through her, both to reinforce her certainty about her startling conclusion as well as to reveal it to the Holts. She wanted to start by asking Winnie's middle name and even debated trying to find it in a public database. She resisted the notion, aware that the more she unraveled, the stronger her desire would grow to discuss it. Considering Azalea's current health crisis, she didn't deem it the proper setting to unseal this time capsule. Even before that, Winnie and Mack had barred her from addressing the earthquake at all.

In an attempt to distract her brain from her spinning theories, she circled back to her original intent to peruse her photos from the day. Instead of browsing through them with her article in mind, however, she continued to search for the way they all fit into her uncle and Nadua's story. Had they kept in touch over the years? Did he realize that she never remarried, despite her brother-in-law's pressure? And if she didn't remarry, why did she and her kids have a different surname from what Uncle Reed called her in the article?

The front door opened, jolting her from her deliberation. Winnie stepped through it, and the calmer expression on her face indicated Azalea's diagnosis wasn't as serious as they feared.

Because of the shuffling of names that had been running through Lorelei's brain, she opted not to use Azalea's—or Nadua's. "How is she?"

"She'll be better after her hip is replaced," Winnie reported. "Her blood pressure and everything is stable, but the X-ray showed a fracture. The doctor said it may have broken and made her fall rather than the other way around. Apparently, that's pretty common for people her age."

"I've heard the same thing," Lorelei agreed. "Good thing she had us with her."

Winnie chuckled at her wink. "Dr. McHenry said that, too. As for her confusion, she seems fine now, so we formed the consensus that the shock of everything just rattled her. She has to go to Anchorage for the surgery, so they'll test her to make sure there aren't any neurological issues otherwise. One encouraging sign was that she told me she has thimbleberry jam in her pantry, and she wants you to take a jar of it home to share with your family."

Lorelei couldn't suppress her grin, and a few goosebumps even popped out on her covered arms. For starters, she hadn't realized Azalea caught her reference to the spread, with her lack of response to it. On top of that, she mused over whether Azalea might be remembering Uncle Reed. She didn't miss the irony that Azalea would give her a sampling without understanding she was his niece...unless she did.

As Winnie collected the jar and some of her mom's necessities for her hospital stay, the gesture paired up with Azalea's other remarks that evening.

"You must be the famous Lorelei," she'd said when she arrived.

"I wish we could've spent more time together, but even in this short span, I think I have the full picture of how delightful you are," she'd expressed in parting.

Both comments struck her as peculiar from the instant Azalea uttered them, but Lorelei rationalized she was just being cordial and ladylike. All the same, it puzzled her that Azalea would've heard much about her from her children, who hadn't been acquainted with Lorelei for very long. What if she was familiar with her through Uncle Reed, over the course of many years?

Once ready to leave, Winnie snapped Lorelei out of her contemplation by employing her assistance to close all of the window shades in hopes of deterring unscrupulous characters. With the doctor calling out an ambulance from the nearest depot to transport Azalea, Mack would pack some clothes and essentials for when he drove up tomorrow. Meanwhile, Winnie and Lorelei could head back, and Winnie would go to the hospital once Lorelei dropped her off at home. After they made it onto the main highway, Lorelei offered to take over the driving so Winnie could update her husband and daughters.

Behind the wheel, she had to snicker inside over the fact that she'd ruminated about Mack's identity on the ride there, and now, she was doing the same about Azalea on the journey back. While Winnie chatted with her family, Lorelei kept trying to trace any breadcrumbs that would further link Azalea with Nadua. Without the photo from fifty years ago in front of her, she summoned it in her mind's eye along with Azalea's current appearance and concentrated on the similarities she already detected. She also gave Winnie a few subtle glances to match her characteristics to Nadua, given she resembled her mom and was a couple of decades closer to the young mother in Uncle Reed's day.

After Winnie concluded her call, Lorelei opened her mouth to ask if Winnie had told Azalea her last name, even if it'd be an odd query. She longed to determine whether Azalea was onto her relation to Uncle Reed. Before Lorelei could make such a fool out of herself, Winnie unwittingly interrupted her.

"Sorry I couldn't wrap that up sooner. I had to transition from daughter duty to mom duty. My oldest, Kyah, was just dumped by her high school sweetheart— via text, to boot. When she told him she might go to college out of state, the insecurity and jealousy bugs conspired against them. She's heartbroken. She tried to call earlier, but I must not have had a good cell signal."

Lorelei apologized for keeping her unavailable, but her ears locked in on Kyah's name, wondering if it was chosen to honor her Uncle Makya. She shelved the curiosity for the moment, instead sharing, "I went through a similar experience. My college boyfriend studied in Australia for a semester, and we broke up within a week of his departure. I'm a pretty free spirit, but even I succumbed to the green-eyed monster. I suppose that's why I never tried long-distance again."

"No matter what, young love is hard," Winnie replied. "Actually, love at any age can be hard."

Lorelei acknowledged the truth in the statement. She reflected on her heartache back then, and with her new insight into Uncle Reed, she better understood his compassion when he comforted her…

She may have been twenty years old, but Lorelei handled her initiation into the world of breakups with the same unashamed mourning as a teenager. Lying face down on her bed, she missed her mom more than ever. She could picture her sitting beside her on the floor, whispering the cliché assurances that her daughter would rediscover love someday as she dried her tears. A sophomore in college, Lorelei shared her dorm with another girl, but already engaged to a handsome senior, her roommate showed indifference to her plight. She merely handed her a box of tissues on her way out to go shopping.

A knuckle rapped on her door, forcing her out of her misery cocoon for the moment. She staggered toward it and put her eye up to the peephole to determine whether she wanted to grant entry to the visitor. Her anticipation of it being a fellow student proved to be wrong, as she found her uncle on the other side. Since no special occasion or parent-visitor day was scheduled for months, she wondered why he would have traveled almost four hours from Sedona to Tucson.

"Uncle Reed," she greeted him. "What are you doing here?"

"I was in the area for a story."

"Oh, really? When did Mountainscape expand its coverage all the way to Tucson?"

"I'm not representing Mountainscape. I'm here on business for the Carmichael Chronicles," he explained with a grin. "My star headliner hasn't been reachable for contact in quite some time."

She allowed a smile to slip out for the first time in the week since her split with Javier. She invited Uncle Reed to step inside and closed the door behind him. "I'm sorry for going AWOL. I haven't been in much of a mood to talk ever since…you know."

She'd told him about their falling-out the night after

it happened, but still angry, she put on a brave front. Now, however, she let her agony show, collapsing into his arms. He remained quiet while she sobbed and stroked her hair like she imagined her mom doing. Continuing to fulfill her dreamy scenario, he showered her with sentiments about *the other fish in the sea.*

He proceeded to recite the metaphor of letting the butterfly go and the possibility of it flying back to you, after which she moaned, "I doubt Javier will give me another chance. I was so stupid and childish for flipping out over him having a girl for a study partner. But that's what brought us together. How can I believe sparks won't fly, when we're half a world apart?"

"You can't. But you also can't rule out the prospect of reconciling one day." He dabbed at her soaked cheeks with a tissue. "My darling, true love resides in hope."

Being a writer, Uncle Reed had a knack for waxing poetic, especially at the children's pivotal impasses. That one rang in her heart more than others, both when she pondered her future relationships as well as considering those of friends. In fact, she often used it in wedding cards, mainly for the acquaintances that, she suspected, just invited her for a gift or were even angling for a deal on a wedding photographer. The message didn't have much of an impact on the outcome of her romance with Javier, aside from revealing to her that they didn't share a true love that hope could save. Still, it taught her the power hope could have if one would manifest it in the right way.

All those years, though, she supposed she'd been writing it with the wrong capitalization, having to assume Uncle Reed had more in mind than the quality.

True love resides in Hope.

He spoke of his true love, residing in a town called Hope.

With her uncle a witty man, she wouldn't put it past him to have a secret double meaning behind the phrase, able to imagine a coy smile crossing his face when she didn't notice. She might have been getting ahead of herself, but she was growing more certain that he remained in some contact with Nadua. What she couldn't figure out was why they never reunited, with their subsequent choices making it clear that they failed to come across a stronger love.

She didn't realize the tears trickling from her eyes until Winnie inquired, "Are you okay?"

Embarrassed, she swiped them away and reached for an adequate excuse. "Yeah, I'm sorry. Like I told you on the way down, my uncle's health has been declining in the past few months, too, so Azalea's scare today just reminded me of my anxieties for him."

"I'm sorry for that. They spend all of our lives worried about us, until they give us reason to worry about them."

"And most people are like you, sandwiched between worrying about parents along with kids." Lorelei tallied that as another advantage to not reproducing. After a silent pause, she resumed their exchange about Kyah, piggybacking off of it to delve deeper into Nadua's identity. "Mack indicated that the meanings of names are very important in your culture. What does 'Kyah' mean?"

" 'Little but wise.' " Winnie's face lit up with pride. "Even as a newborn, my husband and I thought her eyes looked like she was wise beyond her years. Of course, we weren't biased or anything."

"Obviously," she teased. "How about your name?"

"It has several, including 'white, fair, and pure' as well as 'happiness'. Mom said I was her glimmer of happiness after the earthquake."

"I'm sure you were." Lorelei maintained a steady tone, but the notion of Uncle Reed's anticipation of that happiness when he and Nadua selected the name pained her. She swallowed the burning desire to divulge everything, but she permitted one curiosity to escape her lips. "I met a woman called Nadua the other day and thought it was so unique. Any idea what it means?"

Winnie nodded and retained a straight face, but Lorelei didn't miss the subtle sigh that laced her words. " 'Someone found.' "

****

When Lorelei dropped Winnie off at her house, she asked Winnie to keep her apprised of developments on Azalea's surgery. After her companion for the day strode away, Lorelei experienced mixed emotions. Because of her inner grappling about her epiphanies during the ride, the tension inside of her finally abated, relieving her. That relief was accompanied by sadness, however, with her uncertain of her contact with the Holts moving forward. Sure, she would be in the same city as all of them due to Azalea's hospitalization, but should she try to meet up with them again? Even if Azalea had caught on to her relation to Uncle Reed, Winnie and Mack still might be puzzled as to her reason for staying in touch.

Winnie's answer about the meaning of Nadua's name continued to echo in her mind. She couldn't believe how fitting the expression was, both in the past and present. In a cafeteria-turned-shelter filled with earthquake survivors, Uncle Reed had found her and went on to have the most beautiful and tragic love story Lorelei ever read. Now, fifty years later, his niece found her once again, without even seeking her out. History somehow repeated itself, complete with the challenging circumstances that threatened to divide the families yet again.

Back in her hotel room, she plunked her bag onto the desk and continued to process the day's unexpected trajectory as she showered. Once dressed in her pajamas, she sorted through her bag, wanting to put the thimbleberry jam in a secure place for the time being. Truth be told, accepting it spelled trouble from the standpoint of traveling with it, given the TSA wouldn't let her store it in her carry-on. Regardless, she resolved to get it to Arizona one way or another.

While she sifted through the postcards she purchased from Mack, the town's name jumped out of the scenes bolder than it did before. Her brain stumbled on another connection between Hope and her uncle, with it being his idea to call their Alaskan Husky Hope. She grinned and shook her head over the string of correlations to this other side of his life, guessing there were even more she couldn't decipher.

Contrary to the delight and excitement that surged through her earlier that evening, Lorelei's spirits dimmed with each layer that peeled off the onion. Similar to her despondency when she first developed the film, she wondered why her uncle would never share any of this with her, especially if he maintained a relationship with Nadua. She understood why he wouldn't talk about it when they were children and in the event that his romance was as short-lived as she originally concluded. With all that she ascertained in the past few hours, however, she wished he'd included her in this part of his life at some point. Given the way he clammed up when Gabe mentioned the earthquake around her, she couldn't dismiss his silence as an oversight.

After indulging in her pity party for a moment, she put herself in his position, considering how much of her life she would open up about to Harley's kids. Even under the condition of being their guardian, she couldn't imagine relating all of her personal history to them, particularly when it pertained to her love life. Sure, she may use her brushes with heartbreak to comfort a devastated teenage girl through a breakup, but she probably wouldn't take her niece step by step through her past relationships. She doubted most parents would go to such lengths with their own children. No matter how close they were, Uncle Reed had every right to keep his love for Nadua confidential.

Plaguing her most of all, she couldn't decide whether to present her discoveries to him or Azalea. She never wanted him to feel violated over her digging into the film and what it depicted, so she hesitated to take it a bridge farther by revealing that she located the woman in it. She didn't have the powers of persuasion to convince him it was, in fact, through a haphazard series of circumstances beyond her control.

With regard to Azalea, she dealt with the same concerns about overstepping her bounds. If Azalea indeed figured out her identity as Lorelei suspected, she could've inquired about Uncle Reed without divulging anything to indicate their romantic relationship. Instead, she mimicked Uncle Reed, staying utterly silent, save for a couple of hidden innuendoes. How would she react if Lorelei confronted her about their past?

For the next hour, Lorelei buried herself back in 1964, pouring through the entire collection of letters. She yearned for Uncle Reed's writings to guide her in the direction she ought to follow the rest of this winding trail. While they didn't contain a definite answer, each one reinforced his profound affection for Nadua and Makya. Despite all of the obstacles that intimidated her about forging ahead, she would never forgive herself for cowering away from the chance to reconcile them. Too many footholds had materialized before her for her to abandon the path.

So consumed by her soul-searching, she forgot to close the curtains. Past eleven o'clock, the fleeting sun set over eight hours ago. After four days in Alaska, she'd grown used to the almost perpetual darkness that enveloped her surroundings. She rose to shut them, but the fluttering greens and purples that illuminated the sky paralyzed her movements. The Aurora Borealis hadn't made another appearance since she landed, so the breathtaking phenomenon entranced her yet again. On this occasion, she kept her wits enough to nab her camera and begin snapping. Unsatisfied with her shots through the window, she shimmied back into her coat and zipped up her boots over her pajama pants, hastening outside for a better view.

Once she took a couple dozen frames, she ogled without a lens, losing herself in the radiance. The purple tones evoked more thoughts of Azalea, and the greens were reminiscent of Uncle Reed, being his favorite color. She gazed upon their magnificence when they intertwined, but another instant later, they'd split and put on an equally gorgeous show alone.

Lorelei reflected on the fitting representation of the

two, with their lives intersecting for that precious but all-too-brief time fifty years earlier. Though it didn't last, they both preserved their glowing lights, perhaps made brighter by the transient period they spent together.

She could only wish they'd be able to gravitate back to each other and create that beauty once more, for however long they had it.

****

Lorelei slept in later than she had her whole stay, but because of all she already accomplished, she didn't fret much over her schedule. Winnie gave her a few more tips about landmarks she could visit and photograph for comparison images of past pictures of the wreckage. Doli also contacted her with a few other people who were willing to be interviewed if she had time before she departed. While she was at it, Doli gave her another reminder about her desire to read her uncle's article, making Lorelei smile over the woman's persistence.

To her disappointment, she didn't receive any word from Winnie or Mack on Azalea's surgery. Their lack of correspondence didn't surprise her, having anticipated that she would be at the bottom of their list of people to update. With some debate, she opted not to bother them, at least for now. Remembering Uncle Reed's latest health scare, she appreciated how frustrating it can be to have others badgering you for answers when you're still waiting on doctors. She didn't want to add any stress to the family.

Instead, she navigated to the stops Winnie recommended, which showed little of the damage the sites had once suffered. Over lunch, she followed up with Doli's contacts and made arrangements to meet one that evening and another two the next day. Having some free time, she strolled into a nearby shop she'd passed by several times in her travels, before she returned to the hotel.

To make productive use of the rest of her afternoon, she browsed through her photos, not casually, but with a view of shaping her article. She always selected her pictures before she wrote her narrative, aware she was hired for her artistic eye rather than her writing prowess. Weeding out the dismal images, she still had over three thousand remaining on her SD card, without a clue how she'd consolidate it to a three- or four-page piece. She jotted down a memo for future reference to put feelers out to other outlets who may want to incorporate some of the shots she didn't sell to Global Expeditions.

Like Uncle Reed, this experience had grown into so much more than a work trip. Even from the beginning, Lorelei had the ulterior motivation of garnering some insight into Uncle Reed's history, walking the same streets or beholding the same glaciers, if nothing else. The moment she met Mack at the airport, however, something inside her shifted in a manner she'd expected for most of her life but never happened until then…and that was before she learned his probable identity. Although their relationship may not escalate to the heights of Uncle Reed and Nadua's, she floated the idea of whether their ties to the original couple fostered their chemistry.

At the same time, she disregarded the notion that, if matters had worked out between her uncle and his mom, they would've been cousins.

Meeting Winnie and Azalea—Nadua—altered her perspective, as well. She didn't like to admit it to herself, but she contended with a jealousy when Nadua was just a face in a photo and name in letters. Up till she developed that film, she assumed she and Harley were the only family Uncle Reed had. Regardless of her empathy for the widow and her children, she still dealt with that pinch of bitterness over the inkling that someone she didn't know claimed his affections first. Her opportunity to get acquainted with them freed her of those inadequacies, providing clarity of why he held Nadua and Makya so dear.

As Azalea so eloquently put it about her, Lorelei now had the full picture of how delightful they are.

Her heart lighter, she grasped the mug she purchased for Uncle Reed, bewildered by the irony that she bought it without any idea of what Hope already meant to him. She wondered if she should still give it to him. The devious side of her that once spread whipped cream on his pillow while he slept goaded her to do it, as it could've surprised him enough to fess up about his secret love. Her mature, sensitive side warred against that, not wanting to cause him undue pain. The battle thrust her into another round of unresolved questions about the couple's contact through the years along with their current feelings toward each other.

Lorelei attempted to re-center her focus on work, beginning the first draft of her piece. She couldn't get too carried away since she needed to grab a quick dinner before her interview that night. She vacated her hotel room and summoned the elevator, just in time to be alerted that the person she was scheduled to meet wanted to delay the interview another half hour. With it now scheduled for eight o'clock, she anticipated a late night and was glad she took advantage of her slow morning to get some extra winks.

Hating to keep wasting money on takeout, she dropped by a local grocery store to buy enough food to last her for the remaining two days. She figured there was no risk of anything getting too warm in the car, as the thermometer on the dashboard teetered between six- and seven-degrees Fahrenheit. While she couldn't cook in her room, she stocked up on a couple of microwavable meals and prepackaged salads. Before she checked out, the cooler of fresh flowers caught her attention, especially the bouquet crafted with azaleas in it. Tired of fighting the urge, she sent Winnie a text, asking if they needed any groceries or other help she could provide. Without an immediate response, she chose to eat one of the salads in the store's café after she paid, keeping a close eye on her phone as well as the flower arrangement.

Thankfully, she hadn't finished when Winnie replied and caught her up to speed. Azalea's surgeon would operate on her tomorrow, making for a long and monotonous day at the hospital. She declined the offer for assistance, but she extended the casual invitation to swing by anytime she'd like, including the room number. Being all she needed to feel welcome, Lorelei scarfed down the rest of her dinner and cleaned up her trash before she rushed over to purchase the bouquet.

At the hospital, she located the proper floor and consulted the signs to determine the correct way to go. With the room numbers nearing Azalea's, she estimated the room from a short distance away, but she verified it once she approached it. Her eyes and brain did a double-take when she read the number Winnie conveyed, but the name typed into the digital sign didn't match Azalea's. On the contrary, it listed the patient as *N. Macawi*.

An instant later, Lorelei decoded the name and how it validated her theories.

Nadua Macawi.

Feet from her uncle's sweetheart, she paused for a moment to absorb the conclusion of her personal investigation. She assumed Azalea didn't bother to legally change her name but just went by a different moniker. Possible explanations swirled in her mind, but the more important curiosities she had drowned them out. Even so, she couldn't decide whether to inquire about any of them, afraid of inflicting more pain on this fragile woman.

Mack sat in the padded chair beside the bed, where Azalea lay with her weight bearing on her good side. With Winnie nowhere in sight, Lorelei reasoned she might be home with her husband and girls for dinnertime. Mack straightened up from his reclined position, and Azalea switched off the television that featured the evening news. Lorelei apologized for interrupting, but Azalea's gleaming smile upon noticing the flowers made it evident she didn't mind.

"These called out your name," Lorelei teased and handed them to her. "I bet you've heard that line before. I don't pride myself on originality."

Azalea grinned. "Generosity trumps originality any day. Thank you very much."

"You're welcome. A box of chocolates cried out, too, but since Winnie said your surgery's tomorrow, I expected you'd have to fast and didn't want to tempt you."

She nodded. "My loyal son hasn't eaten supper, so he won't make me hungrier."

"I snuck a granola bar while you weren't looking,"

Mack retorted, to which his clever mother wagged her finger at him.

"I have a little while before I need to leave, so I can keep her company if you'd like to go to the cafeteria for a bite."

Azalea agreed, nudging him. "You're skinny enough as it is. The last thing we need is you passing out from starvation."

He gave a few words of protest over the exaggeration but relented. The butterflies in Lorelei's heart woke up when he squeezed her shoulder in gratitude on his way out. She hoped her cheeks didn't blush as she claimed his seat and caught whiffs of his familiar after-shave.

"Are they managing your pain?" she questioned Azalea.

The woman shrugged. "I've accepted the over-the-counter pain relievers, but I always pass on the strong stuff. I'd rather test my tolerance than be doped up."

The blunt reply didn't surprise Lorelei in light of Winnie's statement about her mom's stance of preferring natural remedies. "I don't blame you."

"Well, a lot of people do, but that's never bothered me." Azalea chuckled along with Lorelei. She paused, with her eyes hinting that she had something on her mind. Lorelei was about to pose a follow-up about her surgery, but Azalea spun the conversation away from her health. "Did Winnie give you my jam?"

"Yes, she did. I'm waiting to try it at home, so I don't risk having it spill in my suitcase. I'm looking forward to tasting it, though. Thank you."

"You're welcome. For a long time now, that's been my tradition, to give it to muktuk first-timers. It's a good way to avoid lawsuits!"

Lorelei played along. "Yep, Winnie caught me in the middle of dialing up my attorney."

Azalea snapped her fingers in jest. "Believe it or not, my first 'victim' was another photographer. I'll always remember the disgust on his face, especially when I coerced him to take a few more bites, and he ended up sick! He was such a docile, kind man, but the grimace he wore made me afraid he'd storm off and never speak to me again."

Pretty certain she wanted to enlighten Lorelei but couldn't decide how to go about it, Lorelei made the leap, extracting the photo from where she'd relocated it in her wallet. She held it up to her, a bit thrown by the opportunity to share it with somebody else. "This wouldn't happen to be him, would it?"

Azalea wore both the proud beam of a mother peering at her little boy, as well as the demure glow of a woman in love. She didn't need to utter a word.

Chapter Thirteen

Azalea studied the picture for quite a while. Lorelei remained quiet, not wanting to interrupt her processing. If she and Uncle Reed hadn't kept in contact for all those years, this may have been the first time she gazed at him in decades. Regardless, the image no doubt transported her back to that era of her life. Without realizing it, Lorelei relinquished it to her hand and stared at it with her. Finally, she broke out of her reflection and peered at Azalea, whose tears traced her cheeks.

When Lorelei offered her a tissue, she accepted it and voiced a fraction of her thoughts. "I've always hoped to see this someday. I kept wishing he would send it, but I didn't venture to ask."

Lorelei debated how to respond. After weeks of being the one perplexed by all of this, she was baffled to hold the position of being able to illuminate the past. Still, she wondered if Azalea would be hurt to learn the man she loved never developed it for prosperity. On the other hand, would she appreciate the explanation of his reason for neglecting to share it?

Having spent much time yearning for the truth, Lorelei chose to serve it up but endeavored to do so gently. "He didn't make a copy. I stumbled across it shortly before I came here. I believe it hurt him too much to look back on what he missed. What you both missed. I'm so sorry for taking him from you."

"Oh, sweet girl, you shouldn't apologize for that." She clutched Lorelei's hand and stroked it. "Even though we didn't get to have the life we imagined back then, both of us enjoyed one full of love. I made my way with my kids and treasured our bond, which made the challenges worthwhile. I know you and your brother fulfilled Reed and that he cherished the opportunity to raise you just as much. He's so proud of what you accomplished. He used to send me your pieces."

Lorelei's quivering lips managed to thank her for the touching encouragement. While she attempted to regain her composure, she battled with conflicting emotions again. She hungered for more glimpses into their story after he returned home, but she also had qualms about giving away his silence with regard to her. Up to this point, Lorelei had managed to follow along like he discussed their romance. Would it insult Azalea that he never spoke her name to his family?

With her name in mind, Lorelei continued to edge around the full truth. "Uncle Reed knew you as Nadua. Why do you go by Azalea, if I may ask?"

Azalea sighed, mirroring her daughter's reaction to the name the previous night. " 'Nadua' means 'someone found'. My parents gave it to me because I had a twin brother who was born first, and my mom didn't know she was carrying two babies. So, when her midwife gave her the news that her delivery wasn't over, she birthed me and deemed 'Nadua' a fitting name to denote my unanticipated arrival.

"After the earthquake and especially after your uncle went back to Arizona, I no longer felt found but lost. I kept using it regardless, just because my family and our tribe knew me by it. Once I decided to move us to Hope, I needed a new beginning, so I introduced myself as Azalea. That was always my favorite flower, and Reed bought me a bouquet of them for our wedding. It looked pretty similar to this one."

Chills struck Lorelei, unable to fathom the way history kept repeating itself. At last, she mustered the courage to inquire, "Did the wedding happen?"

She shook her head, like Lorelei presumed she would. "His mom called the hotel we lived in that morning to tell him about the fire. Even without the need to take you guys in, he was in no condition to get married that day. Ever since we met, he'd stood by me and supported me through my grief, so this was my turn to be the strong one. When he told me he'd agreed to provide for you, I urged him to honor that. You needed him."

"But so did you," Lorelei whispered.

Azalea didn't argue the point, but she shed new light on the matter. "Though my brother-in-law and I didn't see eye-to-eye on a lot of things, he helped me raise them, as I knew he would. He kept pressuring me to marry him, but I just put up with it while I needed his support. All the same, I couldn't give in, between my disliking of him and my love for Reed. I still followed his lead when the kids were young, but finally, I'd had enough and brought them to Hope.

"In retrospect, I needed to find myself, rather than continuing to leave that to others. Believe me when I say I cherish your uncle to this day and would have considered it a precious privilege to be his wife if it'd worked out. It baffles me to remember that I didn't even have time after my husband's death to worry about finding love again and a man so willing to nurture my children like they were his own before Reed came along. I will forever be grateful for whatever forces nudged him my way in that cafeteria. But losing him also made me become the strong woman my kids needed me to be."

Numerous questions still coursed through Lorelei, but since none of them truly concerned her relationship with Uncle Reed, she refrained from prying. She couldn't contain the one that did, however. "Why didn't you guys ever reunite, especially after we all grew up? You did keep in touch, didn't you?"

Azalea took a moment to consider the query. "We threw around the idea at various junctions, but I think we both feared that the passage of time and the changes we had to make during it caused us to drift too far apart. Because of my limited resources, we couldn't talk on the telephone, and we didn't even write to each other for three years. After I reached out, we agreed to write a letter once a year on what would have been our anniversary. We toyed with dates and milestones of when we might meet up somewhere, but one obstacle or another always seemed to appear in our path."

Lorelei shoved down the objections that arose in her head over their decision to succumb to such pitfalls, figuring it'd be pointless and maybe wearisome to Azalea. Besides, she understood how the years tended to roll by and consume dreams if one didn't fight it. Even she didn't plan to be unmarried at this point of her life, but the deceptively fast progression of time planted her there.

"Did you tell him about your cancer last year?"

Her gaze grew sad and shifted downward. "No, our annual check-ins ended more years ago than I'd like to admit. He acknowledged that he'd dated another woman a couple of times but that she couldn't measure up to me. Of course, I could relate, never satisfied with anybody other than him, either, but I felt guilty. I was the one who bailed more often than he did on our plans, and I wanted him to open his heart again to the love he deserved, even if it wasn't from me. I decided not to reply to it.

"He sent another note a couple of months later, apologizing if he'd upset me and reassuring me of his devotion, but I didn't respond to that, either. His last one, mailed on our usual day, signaled that he could interpret my message but that nothing would change on his end. Despite my regrets over hurting him, I just forged ahead and convinced myself there was no other remedy but to let him go."

Lorelei struggled not to lash out in defense of her poor uncle. She shuffled through her memories to pinpoint the woman he would've mentioned or any indicator of the heartache he must've experienced after Azalea fell silent. Given he shared Lorelei's rookie articles with Azalea, Lorelei was living on her own by then, and sadly, she didn't keep up with him like she should've. Her ire against Azalea transferred to indignation toward herself for taking him so for granted.

"For whatever it's worth, he didn't get married. I don't recall him getting serious with anyone," she informed her.

Azalea locked solemn eyes with her. "I don't know how much of this you'll share with him, but if you say anything, please assure him I carry him with me every day. In fact, 'Holt' is a name he chose to take if we'd been able to marry. The people in my tribe were so worried my children and I would forsake our heritage if a white man was the head of our household, so he wanted to give us all a Native American name. I didn't jump through the hoops to make it legal, but Mack did. He doesn't have the best relationship with my husband's brother and doesn't enjoy being associated with that side of the family."

"We all have messy parts of our genealogy, don't we?" Lorelei joked. "Does Mack remember him?"

Right on cue, Mack entered the room. "Remember who?"

Lorelei's breath caught in her throat, unsure of how much Azalea would want him to learn. His mom hesitated at first, but she soon presented the photo to him. Lorelei anticipated he'd question who the man was, but he grinned with recognition.

"Pala," he declared, his voice tender.

Lorelei gathered the name must have a significance behind it, and Azalea explained it before she had to ask. "It means, 'like a guardian'."

Lorelei smiled over the term of endearment, before Mack remarked to his mother, "Now, I understand why you dropped your knitting needles when I told you about her."

"I couldn't believe you didn't make the connection. She's a Carmichael from Arizona, who's a photographer," Azalea playfully chided him.

"Well, maybe I would've if you'd let me read those letters he sent every year."

Their banter tickled Lorelei, and she found solace in the knowledge that Uncle Reed had continued to play a part in Mack's life, even in a limited capacity. Considering what a small tot Mack was during their months together, Uncle Reed must've made an impactful impression on him. His decision to assume the name they would've shared as a family touched her that much more.

Mack tried to fill in the gaps he'd missed. "He's your uncle?"

Lorelei nodded her head.

He posed the question Azalea hadn't yet breached. "How's he doing?"

Lorelei glanced at the clock, having stayed longer than she intended to, as it was. She realized discussing his recent diagnosis at length could make her late for her interview, which she'd need to record with her phone because she'd never retain anything after this conversation. Just the same, they deserved the candid honesty that they meted out to her.

"He retired late, only nine years ago, but he loved what he did. He's stayed in pretty good health until the past year, like I mentioned earlier. My brother put him in a nursing home, much to my chagrin, but I'd like to make some adjustments once I get back so I can keep him home. Last month, a neurologist unfortunately diagnosed him with a rare condition called progressive supranuclear palsy."

She summarized the symptoms and prognosis, endeavoring to balance her attention between both of them. Despite her best efforts, she caught her focus slipping toward Azalea, as she was interested in observing her reaction. Deep down, she hoped the sad news would make her reevaluate her refusal to contact him, but with her own scary health battles, she probably would've already done so. Along with that, Azalea didn't need health challenges or older age to reinforce the fragility of life, having witnessed it fifty years ago. Lorelei's heart dropped over the possibility that Azalea had made peace with the prospect of never speaking to

Uncle Reed again, not even to say goodbye.

She had difficulty reading the stalwart lady, as Azalea didn't appear shocked or distressed. In this, she matched Uncle Reed, who didn't let the diagnosis faze him, either. At their age, they both seemed content to accept the ticking clock, though they wouldn't hasten its consequences. Following their decades apart, Azalea may have just been happy to realize he was still out there.

Lorelei stood to indicate her imminent departure, unable to linger much more. With her time around them also dwindling, however, she couldn't stop herself from making a subtle statement that she hoped would resonate with Azalea. "I can't get over the series of events that transpired to allow me to meet you all. I wish I could take the credit, but if I'd had deduction skills like this, I would've taken up investigative journalism."

Mack chuckled. "Well, I expect to be making my share of trips to visit Halyn and Ahanu, so maybe we can reconnect sometime. I've debated looking him up before, but we weren't sure whether he stuck around Sedona."

Though he maintained a casual demeanor, Lorelei registered his pensive cadence and the step he took away from his mom.

As much as she didn't want to make ripples between them, she offered a final reply, "He'd appreciate that. Everybody needs to be found once in a while."

Azalea failed to hide the grin that crossed her lips.

****

A week later, Lorelei sat at her uncle's antique desk and listened to the interview she recorded after her heart-to-heart with Azalea. Living up to her predictions, she'd blanked out the entire exchange, too absorbed in the revelations of the previous hour to focus on the former nurse's account about treating earthquake victims. Thus, the account struck Lorelei as if she was hearing it for the first time, and she could only hope the kind woman hadn't discerned her preoccupation. With the conversation below her own standards, she smacked her forehead more than once, irritated by her lackluster performance.

She continued to sculpt her article and managed to narrow down the shots she'd send Cal, who requested her to give him a bigger sampling than she figured he would want. Surprising her further, he implied that her piece could grow into a special issue of Global Expeditions. The suggestion upped the pressure, but it'd also up the paycheck.

Her deadline remained weeks away, but she strived to finish as much as she could before she began her job at Mountainscape the next Monday. Ever since she landed back in Phoenix, she hadn't slowed down in setting up her affairs to stay in Arizona. Harley gave her some impetus when he picked on her again during the drive home about his doubts that she would follow through with her intentions to put roots down. In an attempt to both prove him wrong and not give herself the chance to accept another job, she marched into her uncle's former workplace and used the pull she had to secure an interview. After that stop, she drove to the nursing home to inform the social worker that she'd be checking her uncle out at the end of the month and caring for him at home. The cooperative man didn't try to discourage her but offered his support in the transition.

She didn't have any agenda to do so, but a few days later, she realized how similar her chaotic return was to Uncle Reed's back in 1964. Within a matter of hours, he transformed from a love-struck bachelor about to walk down the aisle, to a single father figure of two little kids he hardly knew. The comparison strengthened her motivation to repay him for that, as she should have done years earlier.

She put aside her work for now, needing to straighten up the house a bit more before the social worker and an associate from the home health provider arrived to evaluate the place for safety. Although the nursing home couldn't force her not to discharge him, they had to ensure he was going somewhere adequate for his needs. To her gratitude, Harley agreed to help her install grab bars and a couple of other security measures to prevent falls. She welcomed the opportunity to learn any further precautions she could take to keep him comfortable and in one piece.

Stowing away her camera and notes, Lorelei finally removed Uncle Reed's letters from the bag and decided to put them back in his old suitcase, where she'd discovered the film. On top of the stack lay the photo of him with Nadua and Makya, but it wasn't the copy she developed. The day after she and Azalea opened up to each other, she made a copy at a local drugstore, and as hard as it was, she surrendered the original to Azalea. The few weeks she had it in her possession had engendered in her such a sentimental value for it, but how could she lay claim to it over a woman who envisioned it for fifty years? At the same time, she needed a physical copy for herself, not content to just snap a picture of it and relegate it with the thousands of other images in her files.

Azalea showed appreciation for the gesture when she dropped it off, but they didn't engage in another in-depth dialogue like the night before. Having had her surgery earlier that day, she was still tired and recovering from the trauma along with the anesthesia. Beyond that, however, Lorelei picked up on a shared withdrawal among her and her children, as none of them seemed compelled to reopen the past. Not questioning the details of the photo, Winnie appeared to be privy to the story, but she didn't verbalize her opinion. Lorelei related to the toll the medical ordeal had taken on them all, but she worried their mutual admissions strained their feelings toward her.

Even if that was the case, she carried no regrets. Either way, they probably wouldn't have many dealings once she ventured home. At least they all had a sense of closure now...except for Uncle Reed. She wished she'd taken a picture of them together and searched inside herself for the reason she neglected to. Besides the fact that she didn't want to violate Azalea's privacy by requesting her to pose for one in a hospital bed, she hated to have one more thing she couldn't share with Uncle Reed. She'd opted not to regale him with her breakthroughs in Alaska, at a loss on how to confess her invasion into his love life. Without reason to believe Azalea would change her resolve to remain estranged, Lorelei could only imagine that the whole situation would break his heart again.

Underneath the photo she had printed, a sealed envelope slipped out of the stack. For a second, she guessed it had somehow been separated from the rest of Uncle Reed's notes to Gabe, but the size differed from all of the others. Its color wasn't as faded, either. Just before she started to tear it open, she noticed the biggest contrast of all. Rather than having Gabe's address and a postmark on the front, the sender simply wrote *Reed*. Foreign to her, Lorelei pondered how and when it'd been delivered into her bag, until she recalled the long hug Winnie gave her on her way out of the hospital room.

****

Reed propelled his wheelchair with the use of his feet, having refused help from the nurses' aides as he exited the recreation room. He wanted to build up his muscle tone so he'd be as strong and independent as possible at home. At the same time, he took advantage of the social activities available there while he could, realizing his opportunities to play cards and the like would be more limited. He'd scoffed at the hobbies and classes the center offered when Harley first admitted him, deeming them mere preoccupations to distract residents from their inevitable demise. Over the proceeding months, however, he grew to enjoy the variety they afforded his day.

Still, he more than embraced the prospect of retreating home.

Peering around the halls en route to his room, he winced, startled by the sudden boost to his speed. He pivoted his neck to find that his niece had taken over the driving.

"Is this your way of calling me a slow poke?" he teased Lorelei.

"Nah, I like Gabe's nickname for you better, Retired Old Fart!"

He laughed, eager for the loving humor the delightful girl would add to his daily routine. He reckoned they'd have their moments of irritation, too, just like they did during her childhood. It had to be more manageable, though, since she wasn't riddled with teenage hormones and angst now. One thing that needed to remain was his ingenuity for keeping her and her brother separate most of the time.

When they entered his room, she positioned his chair in front of the seat she'd take and engaged the brakes. He told her, "I didn't expect you today, with the inspection and all. I still can't understand what business they have scrutinizing my own house to judge whether or not it's fit for me. I've spent almost sixty years fitting it for myself!"

"Yeah, but that was before I took it over and converted it into a bachelorette pad, complete with a pink hot tub right in the middle of the living room. They told me to install a fence around it so you don't fall in."

He shook his head with a chuckle. "Considering you had to keep your toys in an old toolbox for the first year, I probably deserve it."

"No, you deserve the loving and steadfast care you divvied out." She winked. "In all seriousness, I appreciated the insight from the social workers. They suggested some rearrangements that I'm sure will accommodate us better. The social worker from here even offered to lend us a lift chair until your insurance approves you to get your own."

He grunted. "Anything to keep getting a ration of my money."

Lorelei didn't protest his cynicism. "Well, I had to come to line that up and figured I'd stop in. I also wanted to make a confession about something I found when I recently looked through the attic."

She presented a photograph to him, the one he'd only conjured up in his mind's eye and that appeared in his dreams every so often. The one he was afraid to develop yet popped open its film canister on countless occasions when he ached to see them again. The one he knew he'd cherish if he ever mustered the nerve to give it a permanent place in a frame, the honor it merited.

Over the years, he almost convinced himself it probably wouldn't have been the best shot, anyhow, to ease his sorrow. One of them may have had their eyes shut, and Makya likely stuck out his tongue the way he did when he was bored. In reality, though, the picture encompassed everything he hoped it would and more. Nadua's smile shined so much brighter than it had up to that point in his trip. Despite physical fatigue from the late stage of her pregnancy and her emotional weariness from the tribe's ridicule about their relationship, she had just told him she still chose him. He hadn't yet proposed marriage, but he very much embraced the prospect and already deemed her and her children as his own.

Makya wasn't in the habit of posing for photos, having given Reed trouble every time he tried to take one of him. Reed bubbled with pride over his charming gaze into the lens for this one and the adorable smile on his lips. More than anything, his expression showed trust and safety as he leaned against Reed's leg, a different boy from the scared toddler he met in the makeshift shelter. All these years later, Reed's pain over having to strip away that newfound security had yet to fully heal.

Regardless, the little boy's calls echoed through his head as if the tot stood beside him. *Pala, come here.*

Lost in the image and the heartrending story behind it, he just about forgot about his niece sitting across from him. He predicted the barrage of questions she'd ask and braced himself to have to admit everything...including why he'd kept this part of his past a mystery. Stalling, he reverted to their playful repartee. "I don't know if I ought to scold you more for snooping or for using a store to develop the film."

"I apologize for my nosiness, but with regards to the film, I processed the original print in your darkroom. I made a copy before I gave it to Nadua."

He couldn't stop his jaw from slacking. "You what?"

Rather than demanding explanations from him, Lorelei provided him with a plethora of them. She recounted her run-in with the photographer in the terminal and then her meeting the history professor from Hope. She told him about the twists that took her to the small town—whose zip code he still remembered—topped off by her getting acquainted with the quiet but impish woman named Azalea Holt. The sound of her adopted name sprang tears in his eyes, but they dissolved into laughter when Lorelei shared her introduction to muktuk.

"To this day, that horrible aftertaste lingers in my mouth!" Reed claimed. "I'll bet she laughed at you the same way she did me."

Lorelei nodded. "Along with the rest of the restaurant. To her credit, she followed through with another of her tricks."

She dug into her purse and extracted a bag with a couple of slices of bread, as well as a jar of jam. He snickered. "Let me guess—thimbleberry."

His niece confirmed it, even prepared with a knife and disposable plates. She spread the treat over his piece and handed it to him, before she made up her own. Taking a bite, he relished getting reacquainted with the unique flavor, and he couldn't believe how long it had been since he first tried it. After that many years, one would think his taste buds would register the tarty tang as foreign, but instead, they anticipated its texture and different undertones that it emitted as he chewed. More than anything, however, he craved the company he associated with it.

With it being Lorelei's initial sampling, he observed her reaction, able to discern that she savored it, too, from the glimmer of joy in her eyes. While they ate together, he began to contemplate why he'd refrained from telling her everything ages ago. For many years, he kept it to himself because it was all too painful to discuss, and as young as she and Harley were, they wouldn't have any interest in it if he did open up. Once they would've understood, he feared making either of them question their worth to him or planting doubts about his willingness to take care of them. In light of the conversation he had with Lorelei just the other night when she asked him about the sacrifices he made, he gathered she contended with such inadequacies even as a grown woman.

Regardless, he wished deep down that he had shared some of his and Nadua's story with Lorelei, at least. She, Nadua, and Makya each held a big portion of his heart, and it refreshed his soul to finally have the walls separating them fall down. In retrospect, he always hoped to get to this point when he and Nadua could rekindle their love and start anew, but that occasion never came.

As his head continued to swirl, it occurred to him to ask Lorelei, "How did you know to look for Nadua in the first place?"

"Well, for one, I developed the picture before I left.

When that piqued my interest, I employed your former editor, and after some maneuvering on my part, he entrusted me with the drafts of your article. In my professional and unbiased opinion, every one of them is worthy of being published, but we'll get into that later."

"Who knew Benedict Arnold spelled his name G-A-B-E?" Reed replied. He opted not to inquire whether or not his friend included the letters he sent with the drafts. If he didn't, bringing that up would only serve to heighten her insatiable curiosity. For now, he wanted to quench his thirst for more insight. "How is she?"

Lorelei paused to put away the jam and crumple up the bag that had held the bread, before she retrieved an envelope from her purse. She placed it in his hands and began to stroll out of the room. "I'll let her tell you."

Once alone, he opened it, and his breath caught upon perusing her beautiful handwriting.

My Beloved Reed,

I've begun this letter time and again but haven't ever been able to finish it. Considering everything you and the memory of you have done for me, I've often felt unworthy of the opportunity to right matters. I'm so sorry for shutting you out like I did, but please understand I really believed it was in your best interests. You deserved the unwavering love you showed me, and the woman I was back then couldn't return it. On the other hand, you deserved a fair explanation and closure, if nothing else, and I should've given you that.

My lack of correspondence in no way reflects my lack of devotion. I think of you every day, during the happiest milestones and the most difficult travails. Since we met during the hardest one of my life, I used to wonder if my heart deemed you a mere life jacket,

229

Karina Bartow

someone to turn to when I was at my worst. Those doubts scared me and contributed to my choice to give you up. Over time, I've realized how unfounded they were and that my love for you is rooted far deeper than that.

At Winnie's wedding, my imaginings fluctuated between visions of Matto and you here. I pictured him walking her down the aisle, but I imagined you dancing with her at the reception. I've done the same and more while watching Mack's various achievements, especially when he's behind the camera, and I'm forever grateful for your influence on him at that tender age. I worried so much that he would forget you, but he never has.

As much as I miss you during the big moments, I feel your absence even stronger through the small, mundane ones. I can't express how often I've longed for your compassionate insight to guide me through a decision, your listening ear to appreciate my sense of humor that few people consider funny, and your loving arms to warm me. At the same time, I yearned to be able to support you, whether it be with caring for the children, nudging you to put more stock in your infinite talents, or broadening your culinary horizons!

Your dear Lorelei's visit showed me that you capitalized your opportunity to be their father figure exactly like I expected you to, and it paid off. Even without my intervention, she seems to have an adventurous palette and resilient stomach to go with it! In all seriousness, just a few hours with her enriched me the same way you always did. I can tell you instilled much of your values, generosity, and heart in her, which gives me peace beyond measure.

Her unusual arrival also underscored that it's never too late to make amends. No matter how hard I try, the universe seems intent that I can't let you go. At this point in our lives, I'm not sure if a future together is conceivable, but I'm done running from the gravity that draws us to each other. I think the love we've shared even in silence has carried us through our ups and downs, so don't we both deserve to give it a voice again?

Forever Yours,

Nadua

Beneath her poignant words, she included her phone number. After he wiped away his tears, he marveled again at the photo of him, Nadua, and Makya, tracing them with his fingers. He took a deep breath and began to dial.

Epilogue

2024

Lorelei waltzed into the downtown Anchorage gallery, fighting the urge to pinch herself. During her long career, she never aspired to have her work showcased in an exhibit, but she couldn't deny the gratification the occasion endowed in her. Accustomed to her photographs being reduced to fit in a magazine collage or centerfold at best, she almost giggled like a child when she stood before her shots, blown up to hang on the wall. As she meandered through the space and viewed them one-by-one, the nostalgia from ten years ago rushed through her, still awestruck by what that single assignment contributed to her world.

Sponsored by the university—primarily Winnie's department—the commemorative art show featured several artists' depictions of the earthquake. The paintings Winnie had on display at the library when Lorelei first visited hung nearby, and Lorelei enjoyed the chance to meet the artist behind them at last. They'd chatted briefly on the phone for her Global Expeditions article, but here, she appreciated getting to discuss his pieces and her admiration for them in greater detail.

Afterward, she moseyed to the middle of the gallery, where a standalone wall served as the centerpiece of the exhibit. Of course, Winnie's part in the selection process tipped the scales, but even without her influence, Uncle

Reed's photos anchored the expanse in the most incredible way. The ones of the devastation in the quake's aftermath contained such a personal quality to them that few of the more famous images did. Based off the reactions from the guests who'd begun to trickle in, the shots shed new light on the tragedy's impact.

Along with such messages, the addition of his and Nadua's love story attested to the joy that could triumph heartbreak. The portrait that remained unseen for half a century was enlarged bigger than many of the other pieces, with a placard beside it that highlighted their account. Alongside that were pictures of their life following their reunion, including the first one they took when Nadua visited after her new hip healed and their wedding photo four months later.

As she stood and admired the gorgeous tribute, a pair of familiar arms enveloped her waist, with a bouquet of azaleas placed into her arms. She spun toward her husband, who kissed her cheek before he took her side and joined her in her musing. She sniffed the flowers, with the scent reminiscent of the bunch Nadua carried on her wedding day and the one Lorelei held at her own eight years ago.

She complimented Mack on his choice. "What a fitting gift for tonight."

"Yeah, I considered an arrangement of reed stalks, but the florist didn't share my vision," he joked. "I wish they could've been here to experience this."

"So do I."

Lorelei swallowed the lump in her throat that kept reforming. Within minutes, Winnie entered the building with her family, soon followed by Halyn and her husband with Ahanu and his little brother, Reed, in tow.

Right behind them, Harley and Genevieve wandered in with their four children, having flown in for the event, too. She greeted the families, and they toured the sixtieth anniversary commemoration together. When they rounded the display that honored Uncle Reed and Nadua, a stillness prevailed among them, each of the adults cherishing the memories the shots captivated.

Despite how strongly she missed them both, she remained grateful that they had the chance to spend their final years side-by-side. She believed Nadua's presence delayed the progression of Uncle Reed's illness, with him being spared the worst symptoms of supranuclear palsy. Likewise, Nadua maintained decent health, steering clear of a recurrence of cancer. In their six years as husband and wife, they enjoyed a couple of returns to Alaska, countless hours laughing with Ahanu, and Uncle Reed's opportunity to give Lorelei away at her nuptials.

While she observed her uncle's work receiving the high praise it deserved, a part of her felt sorrow over how many accomplishments he celebrated with her, but he missed his turn to shine. Even so, she realized how he would react to it, recalling the day her article—and his— came out in Global Expeditions...

She remembered her heart swelling with pride when the magazine arrived in their mailbox. Though she'd viewed the proof before it was published and the online edition of the issue that subscribers received yesterday, nothing beat the sensation of holding the print copy in her hands. She hadn't soared with such glee over a publication in ages, used to the honor by now. In this case, however, her elation concerned more than her. She couldn't wait for her uncle to behold his name on a byline in the renowned periodical, as it should have been long before today.

Having moved home three months prior, Uncle Reed was busy doing his exercises with his home physical therapist, as he did everything he could to stay agile around the house. She resisted her urge to interrupt them, deciding to wait the forty minutes before their session would conclude. To settle her excited nerves, she flipped through the issue and read over his contribution again, pleased with the way they combined several of his drafts to compose a beautiful piece that was as relevant now as it was when he penned it.

She'd coerced him to allow her to show his article to Cal for his consideration, but she didn't tell him the editor approved to include it. Before the therapist pulled out of the driveway, then, she bounded into Uncle Reed's room to share the surprise with him.

She held up the cover. "Look what finally turned up!"

He congratulated her like usual, with his eyes twinkling with pride. She chose not to skip right to his feature, preferring him to stumble across it organically, but she became antsy when he took his time scanning through her pictures and headlines. She pointed out that he already browsed through them all with her and even assisted her with editing. Nonetheless, he scoured each page with keen interest.

At last, he made it to his write-up, but to her astonishment, he released a simple, "Huh," over the sight. He skimmed over his work, critiquing his younger terminology and camera angles as if he were exploring an old family album.

"Really?" Lorelei couldn't suppress her irritation over his cavalier manner. "That's all this means to you?"

He extended his hand to cover hers. "Don't get me wrong, sweetheart. I'm honored by the acknowledgment and what you did to make it happen. But in the grand scheme of things, this isn't the pinnacle of my lifetime."

"Maybe not, but I reckoned you'd be a little more thrilled. This was your dream way back when you went to Alaska. I understand why you were reluctant to profit off of somebody's trauma once you witnessed the devastation, but still, not many journalists get to read their name in Global Expeditions. Even without my input, I'm convinced you would've earned this."

Uncle Reed grinned. "I appreciate your confidence in me more than you know. Let me clear something up for you, though. Yes, it did strike me a few days into my trip that the survivors were pummeled by loss and misery, and here, I was just focused on gaining momentum for my career. It altered my perspective on priorities and motivated me to get involved, rather than just stand by and report. But I proceeded with my writing, even after I'd fallen in love with Nadua, because I knew it was an important story that needed to be told.

"That said, the experience taught me that you don't have just one purpose in life. You can have several, and they usually change over time. Sure, I thought my purpose would be to net awards, and then for a short time, it became taking care of Nadua and Makya, before it shifted to you guys. I never resented that redirection, and not once did I languish over a void those changes opened up. Obviously, it called for adjustments, and I always hoped matters would align for Nadua and me again. In the meantime, I embraced my current purposes, without investing much energy in *what could've beens*."

While the sentiment and its lesson moved her, she

couldn't resist teasing him. "Yet you held onto a roll of film full of *what could've beens* for fifty years."

"Like I said, I didn't waste time looking back," he replied. "That is, until my nosey niece stormed into town!"

"I'm going to take that as a compliment. Since this didn't blow you away like I intended it to, maybe my gift will. I planned to wait until Nadua arrives, but I've had enough of surprises."

He untied the ribbon on the present she handed him. When he yanked out the instant camera inside, he scowled in confusion, until the message resonated.

She winked. "To keep you from leaving any more undeveloped mysteries for me!"

With one of the few snapshots he permitted her to take with the bargain model featured in the collection, Lorelei drew her family's attention to it, laughing. Winnie and Harley reveled in the humor of it, too, but a student reporter interrupted the moment when she requested an interview with Lorelei for the university's newsletter. Happy to oblige, she stepped away from the group, finding it odd to be the one answering the questions rather than asking them.

The young woman issued several queries about her experience as well as Uncle Reed's. She ended the brief exchange by inquiring, "What's the main takeaway you want visitors to gain from this?"

Lorelei considered her response for a beat, endeavoring to speak for Uncle Reed and Nadua, besides herself. "No matter how the earth or your personal world may shake, find your stability in hope."

A word about the author...

Karina Bartow grew up and still lives in Northern Ohio. Though born with Cerebral Palsy, she's never allowed her disability to define her. Rather, she's used her experiences to breathe life into characters who have physical limitations, but like her, are determined not to let them stand in the way of the life they want. She may only be able to type with one hand, but she writes with her whole heart! http://www.karinabartow.com

Thank you for purchasing
this publication of The Wild Rose Press, Inc.

For questions or more information
contact us at
info@thewildrosepress.com.

The Wild Rose Press, Inc.
www.thewildrosepress.com

www.ingramcontent.com/pod-product-compliance
Lightning Source LLC
Chambersburg PA
CBHW070108030726
47506CB00002B/639